THE BLUERIDGE JUNCTION BOYS

CAN'T FIGHT IT

LEVI & JAY

A.D. ELLIS

WWW.FACEBOOK.COM/ADELLISAUTHOR

A.D. Ellis WEBSITE

COVER, SPINE, BACK BY

KAY SIMONE

at

Kay Simone Creative

QUOTES OF INSPIRATION

"It is a risk to love. What if it doesn't work out? Ah, but what if it does?"

~Peter McWilliams

DEDICATION

To small towns and the people who love them, hate
them, love to hate them, and hate to love them.

INTRODUCTION

I fell in love with the male/male romance genre back when I wrote my first one (<u>Sawyer, Torey Hope: The Later Years</u>) and couldn't wait to write the six books in my male/male romance series <u>Something About Him</u>. As the most recent series was coming to an end, I started to wonder what I would write next.

I grew up in small farming community with a railroad running only about four houses down from where I lived, so small towns and railroads are familiar to me. My mind started playing with the idea of these three men (Micah, his cousin Levi, and their best friend Cody) growing up on a hill in this small railroad town. *Blueridge* was the name that came to me. Well, then my head started playing with words and landed on nicknaming the series The BJ Boys, so I created Blueridge Junction and the rest is history.

These three stories combine some of my very favorite male/male romance tropes.

Fight for It is a tale of a mechanic and a teacher in an out-for-you tale. (Grab Fight for It on Amazon if you've not read it yet.)

Can't Fight It is a story of opposites attract and May/December romance.

Bound to Fight combines the best of leather daddies and enemies-to-lovers for a great story.

CAST OF CHARACTERS

Micah Edwards- Mechanic in Blueridge Junction, cousin of Levi, best friend of Cody.

Cole Pierce- Teacher at the high school

Levi Wells- Tattoo artist in Blueridge Junction, cousin of Micah, best friend of Cody

Jay Owens- Dancer at Strip Teaze, much younger than the rest of the guys

Cody Parker- Manages his family-owned restaurant/bar (BJ's Burgers & Beer or the B & B) Friends with Levi and Micah

Kennedy Marks- Local police officer in Blueridge Junction

CHAPTER 1

LEVI WELLS

His mouth was every bit as sweet as I'd known it would be.

The way he drank from my lips, and put his whole body into the kiss, lit a fire in my already heated blood. I'd waited so long, but no more. Allowing my hands to roam down his back to grip his ass, I pulled him flush against me. Our hard cocks rocked together, and I silenced his whimper with my mouth.

When he tugged at the hem of my shirt, urging me to remove it, I released all hesitation. We'd waited too long; the heat too much. I pulled the shirt over my head and groaned as his graceful hands trailed over my naked skin.

Fear surfaced that I could break this beautiful boy was still there, but I reveled in everything about his gorgeous lithe body. His shorter height put his mouth closer to lick and tease my nipples. His smaller frame allowed me to wrap my arms around him as a protector. His pale, perfect, unmarked skin was a stark contrast to my heavily tattooed body. His light brown floppy shock of hair was perfect for running my hands through while he ran gentle fingernails against my shaved head.

"More, please."

His breath came in pants and his words were a plea I couldn't ignore. Stripping the shirt from his body, I marveled at the slim yet muscular dancer's physique under my hands. Graceful, smaller, and almost fragile looking, yet the muscles flexing and stretching under my touch told another story.

When he fumbled with my pants, I stepped back in hopes of pausing the speed of what was happening between us. But, he hooked his thumbs in my waistband and my boxer briefs before slowly peeling them down my legs. My weeping cock sprang up.

The kid licked his lips and dropped to his knees, and all thought of slowing down stampeded from my head. His soft pink tongue tasted me, seemingly hesitant at first, but he soon wrapped his kiss-swollen lips around my dick.

I'd dreamed of the moment for months upon months, but never believing I'd have him. But, as he sucked my cock with those gorgeous brown eyes staring up at me, I knew dreams could come true.

Gripping fists full of his hair, I thrust my shaft slow and deep into his greedy mouth. When one hand cupped my balls and the other teased my ass, I knew I wouldn't last long. "Gonna come," I warned.

He squeezed my balls and probed my hole as he hummed around my cock.

My release slammed through me like a freight train, nearly bringing me to my knees. I watched him swallow every last drop of me.

Pulling from my cock, he stood and reached for his shirt as if we were finished.

"Oh no you don't. We aren't done here." I kissed him hard, savoring the mix of his sweet and my salty, while I backed him to the couch. Swiftly removing his pants and underwear, I gently pushed against his chest. Dropping to my knees, I admired his dick. Everything about the kid was beautiful. Licking up the seam of his balls, I immediately took his throbbing shaft so deep into my mouth that my nose nuzzled against his lower belly.

His hips rocketed up, thrusting deeper as I swallowed around him. Testing the weight of his balls in one hand, I reached a finger of the other up to his lips urging him to suck it. When it was wet enough, I sucked him, cupped his balls again, and teased my slick finger against his hole.

"Someday, soon, I'll be in here. My big, fat cock drilling your tiny pink hole until you come all over yourself." My rough and dirty words shocked me, but he whimpered and fucked my mouth over and over.

Gripping his cock, I trailed my tongue to his ass and swirled it around his pucker in tandem with my finger. Dip of the tongue, press of the finger, and a kiss against his most sensitive spot. I repeated the series three times before he let loose, groaning my name and shooting his load all over his stomach and chest. I worked my way up, cleaning him with my lips and tongue, until I met his mouth. Kissing him, I thrilled at how his hungry mouth sipped and savored mine until our flavors mingled.

"Mmm, I can't wait until you're fucking me for real, *Daddy*."

His words teased and taunted, and his all-too-familiar nickname excited as much as irritated. "Felt pretty damn real to me," I growled against his ear.

His answer was as loud and shrill as a passing train whistle.

No, his answer actually *was* a loud, shrill passing train whistle.

What the fuck?

I jerked back to look for him and saw only darkness. The only thing real in that moment was the train rumbling through the night.

Covered in sweat and tangled in my blankets, I came to the stark realization that I'd once again dreamed of him.

Of Jay.

Jay Fucking Owens.

"Every damn night." I ran a rough hand over my face before grasping my trembling cock. I'd spent myself all over the sheets. "Like a fucking pre-teen having a damn wet dream. You are one messed up motherfucker." I spoke harshly as I rolled from the bed and stripped the sheets. Walking naked to the laundry room, I started a load before making my way to the bathroom for what was becoming a regular late night shower routine.

Standing under the steamy spray, I chastised myself once again for the dreams I couldn't control. The only positive of coming all over myself like a damn horny teen was I'd done it while asleep and didn't have to wrestle with my conscious over whether or not it would be okay to jack off to the image of Jay sucking my cock in the shower.

Once cleaned up, I put a clean set of sheets on the bed. I'd need to get a few new sets, because this nightly laundry shit was for the birds. Pulling on a loose pair of boxers, I climbed into bed and attempted to settle my body and my mind. Sated and relaxed from my previous *activity* and the warm shower, my body calmed almost instantly.

My mind, however, was hopping. And, as with most nights, my thoughts went straight to Jay.

The damn kid had shown up in Blueridge Junction when he was just a few months shy of his nineteenth birthday. Jay Owens was a walking stereotype of a gay man. Campy, flashy, flamboyant. And absolutely gorgeous. He worked as a dancer at the local gay bar on the outskirts of town, Strip Teaze. Rumor had it that he'd come to Blueridge Junction, or BJ as the locals called it, to flee a less-than-positive home life. He followed me around like a lovesick puppy for two years, batting his kohl-lined eyes and pouting his perfect pink lips in hopes of catching my attention.

And he caught it all right. Much to my chagrin.

At over ten years the kid's senior, I had no right to be lusting over someone so much younger. Granted, Jay was turning twenty-one within a few days, but he wasn't even my type. I liked my men firm and tough, not slim and fragile. I wanted a man I could tumble into bed with, not a kid who looked as if he'd blow over with a strong breeze.

But, for two years, I'd fought the pull. I'd fended off his ridiculous advances. I'd ignored the tightness in my pants when Jay showed up with his nails painted and his face all made up. I pretended it didn't bother me to think of horny men groping at him and tucking bills in his shorts as he moved his gorgeous body around the stage. I scoffed at his insistence on calling me *Daddy* when inside all I could think about was holding him in my arms and making him mine, making him scream my name, and showing him who his *daddy* really was.

"God damn, you're a fucking sick ass pervert, Wells." I tossed and turned, trying to think of anything but Jay.

But, instead, I thought of his slight build, his almost wispy appearance, and the fact that the kid was constantly hungry and looking for something to eat. My heart went out to him. Despite all the things that drove me insane, I considered him a friend. He had gotten very close to my cousin, Micah, and Micah's boyfriend, Cole. Jay spent some of his free time helping Micah at the auto shop. And, by *helping,* I meant chatting while Micah worked on whatever car was in the bay at the time. Jay was maybe closest to Cole. Cole hadn't been in town as long as Jay, but he'd been through a pretty rough time. Jay had befriended Cole when Cole's job as a local high school social studies teacher was in jeopardy due to Cole's sexuality. Micah and Cole were grateful for Jay's support. In fact, they loved the kid. Which irritated and warmed my heart at the same time.

My best friend, Cody's personal mission was making sure Jay got extra food whenever we were all in BJ's Burgers & Beer. Cody and his family owned and managed the restaurant. Hell, even our local law enforcement friend, Kennedy Marks, had taken it upon himself to watch out for Jay.

Sighing heavily, I listened to the lulling roar of the passing train down at the junction. The train cars were usually clanking loud during the day when the tracks and cars were switched and moved. But, at night, the trains that passed through BJ were like a lullaby to my soul.

I'd lived in BJ my entire life. My house sat on Blueridge Hill with three other family's homes. Micah's family, the Edwards, had been in Blueridge Junction as long as my own. Cody Parker's family had resided on the ridge for almost the same amount of time. Micah's father was recently deceased, his mother, Susan, was living with Hank and Marian

Parker, and Micah and Cole were currently living in my guest house until their own home was finished being built on Blueridge Hill. Cody and his sister, Sadie, lived on the Parker property with their parents. With both of my parents deceased, I appreciated having family and friends nearby.

Before sleep overtook me completely, I thought once more about Jay. The attraction between us would have to be ignored. As a local tattoo artist, I had a reputation to uphold in the community. I couldn't been seen as a cradle robber. Plus, the feelings I had toward Jay were lustful only, it wasn't as if I wanted to *date* him. He was an itch that wouldn't get scratched. Maybe I'd check out that dating app and find someone more age appropriate and more my type. I needed to forget about Jay Owens.

Convincing myself of that wasn't going to be easy.

Convincing Jay of moving on from me was going to be even harder.

Especially when we saw each other practically every day because of our circle of friends.

The draw between us had gotten stronger as the years had gone on and I'd gotten to know him better. But, it was a force I'd have to fight. I was a grown man; I could fend off a lustful attraction to a breathtaking young dancer.

Right?

I'd have to.

No way could the kid and I have anything even remotely resembling a relationship.

My phone buzzed with a notification. *Reminder: Birthday party for Jay*

Shit. How had I agreed to have the party at my house? It made sense. I lived alone and had plenty of room. But, asking Jay to come to my house was sort of like inviting the fox into the hen house.

And, of course, Jay had declared himself the official party planner for his own birthday. Saying he didn't trust such an important life event to be overseen by anyone but the birthday boy himself. Jay had assigned everyone a job and presented us with personalized gift ideas. Plus, he'd insisted on being in charge of decorations. Though I feared what Jay would do to my house, I'd agreed to host the party.

I had two days to get through appointments at the tattoo shop. Then, Friday night at midnight, I knew the party would officially start. Jay's actual birthday was Saturday, but at one minute after twelve, Jay wanted to have his first *legal* drink. He planned on the party taking up all of Saturday and into Sunday. I was likely the only person not totally stoked about the party.

But, like it or not, Jay Owens would show up at my house on Friday evening to decorate his little heart out. And I'd probably end up with teeth ground down to the gums from fighting off the sensual images of him. Why had I ever agreed to this? Damn Jay Owens.

CHAPTER 2

JAY OWENS

"I think the streamers are perfect. Let's get the beads strung up." I tossed a bag of pink beads to Cole.

Pink streamers adorned the top of every single doorway and each hallway in Levi's house.

"Beads too? Maybe 'less is more' in this instance?" Cole scrunched his nose as he glanced around the partially decorated house.

"No way. It's my birthday party. My *twenty-first* birthday party. The theme is 'Pretty in Pink.' More pink is definitely better in this case." I danced Cole into the kitchen. "We'll start the beads here. I want at least two doorways filled with beads." After exiting the kitchen, I returned in dramatic fashion, pretending to walk through beads. "I want to watch Levi emerge from the beads every damn time he enters and leaves the kitchen."

Cole shook his head and rolled his eyes. Which was the same reaction Micah, Cody, and Kennedy all had each and every time I spoke of my undying love and affection for Levi Wells.

"You know, you've been in Blueridge Junction for two years and Levi hasn't once responded to your clear-as-day come-ons. Maybe you two are meant to be just friends." Cole winced apologetically over his shoulder as he stretched to attach the beads to the top of the doorway.

"Only *you*, Cole Pierce, could get away with speaking to me of such horrid things." I cocked my hip, placing a fist upon it. "Levi and I are meant to be amazing, fabulous, and so damn cute people won't know whether to say 'Awwww' or puke their guts up."

Cole laughed. "That's descriptive." Returning to his task, he continued. "I'm just saying. Maybe there's too much stacked against you. He's ten years older than you, claims you're not his type at all, and hasn't shown the slightest interest despite your best efforts."

"Cole, if I've said it once, I've said it a million times. I don't care how much Levi tries to fight it, I'm not giving up. He can't fight what's between us. Well…he *can* try, but he won't succeed." I shrugged, not in the least bothered that no one else thought I stood a chance in hell with Levi. "He's exactly my type. I love the strong, rough kind. His tattoos, his maturity, his stubborn personality…all of those things call to me and make me more determined each and every day to make that man mine."

"So, let's say you reach your goal? Then what? You snag him, you two fuck each other out of your systems, and then? Is it the chase? You like to tease?" Cole paused in his bead work. "I want you happy, but what if you're placing too much hope on this one guy? What if you finally get your man and then it's a huge crash and burn when the two of you go your separate ways?"

I simply smiled and shook my head. "No, no, no, my dear Cole. You don't get it. I'm not after Levi for a few hookups. The thrill of the chase is great. The teasing is fun; lord how I love to tease that man. But, it's more than that. All the teasing and that aside, *nothing* has made me feel like what I feel when I'm around Levi. He makes me feel safe. I feel like he sees me for more than a pretty face and body."

Cole cocked his head. "Are you saying you intend to make a relationship with Levi? Like a full-blown, boyfriends with a future type thing?"

"It's what I've seen between us since the moment I arrived in BJ." I nodded. I knew the other guys didn't get it, but I knew in my heart that Levi and I were meant to be.

"The man is drop-dead gorgeous, I'll give you that. And, he's a great tattoo artist and overall good guy." Cole gave me a look that bordered on pity. "But, has he ever given you any indication that he's into you? You're stunningly beautiful." Cole rolled his eyes as I batted my lashes and preened. "Anyone would be justified in finding you attractive, so I'm sure he has no qualms over admitting he's attracted to you. But, into you like *into* you? He's irritated by you most of the time, hates your teasing, and basically bounds from the room as soon as you're too close."

"Exactly." I smiled triumphantly.

"Exactly what?" Cole huffed and threw up his hands.

"The man has it bad for me. At first, it was a physical attraction. And, if it had stayed at that, Levi likely could have ignored it and fought the pull. But now," my hands flew in a flourish to my sides, "he's attracted to me as a person. He's watched me grow up. He sees me with his family and friends. He knows my personality, my flaws, and my fabulousness." I walked over to Cole and put my arm around his shoulders. "You see, Professor, Levi is falling hard and fast. It's inevitable. His gut instinct is to hate when I call him *Daddy*, but deep down he only hates that he loves it. Mark my words, he's irritated for sure, but it's not truly irritation at *me*. He's angry with himself for wanting me, liking me, finding himself thinking about me and not being able to escape."

"So, you're going to capitalize on his anger and irritation and go in for the kill when he's at a weak point?" Cole turned questioning eyes my way. "That doesn't seem like a great way to begin any relationship."

"Oh no, I'm doing nothing of the sort." I shook my head and smiled deviously. "I'll continue on as my irresistible self until Levi finally acquiesces and realizes he can't fight what's between us."

"It's been two years," Cole reminded me.

"I'm a patient man. No worries." I shrugged again. "Now, we've got *a lot* more pinking to make this party pretty in pink. Let's get to it."

~*~*~

"Honey, I'm home!" I shouted as I walked into Levi's tattoo parlor.

A very disgruntled and hot-as-hell Levi came from the back drying his hands on a paper towel. The shop smelled of ink, soap, and disinfectant. Levi took pride in keeping his business clean and professional looking. As he came closer, I smelled the faint lemon soap on his skin. The scent reminded me of sunshine and Levi, two things I'd never get tired of.

"Damn it, Jay. I've told you not to yell things like that when you come in here." Levi tossed the towel in the trash. "What if I'd been with a client?"

I pouted and batted my lashes. "I'm sorry. I did look to make sure there wasn't a car in the lot other than yours."

Levi shook his head and checked his watch. "What are you doing here? I thought you were decorating for your birthday party."

"Cole and I finished a while ago. It's all ready. I thought I'd come visit to pass the time." I sauntered into Levi's office and hopped onto his desk.

"I've got a client coming soon."

Levi's words were a warning, but I paid them no attention. He followed me into the office and frowned at my perch on his desk.

"That's okay. We can chat until they get here." I swung my legs from the desk and stared at Levi. I knew I looked good, and I knew Levi had noticed. The more growly the man got around me, the more I knew he was affected. I bit my lip and smiled. "So, did you get my birthday gift?"

Levi took an exasperated breath and pulled a piece of paper from his pocket. "No, I did *not* get you," he glanced at the list I'd given him and blushed before continuing, "butt plugs, a blind fold, condoms, or new jocks." Folding the list back up, he shoved it in his pocket.

I couldn't help but chuckle at how off-kilter Levi was. "That's okay, those were just suggestions."

"Did you give the same list to everyone?"

"Oh god, no." I winked. "That one was special just for you."

"Lucky me," Levi sighed. "Seriously, why are you here?"

"I want a tattoo," I quipped.

"You've been asking for a tattoo since you came to town two years ago. My answer is still no." Levi frowned and checked the time on his phone.

"I'm twenty-one now. No one can say I'm not fully an adult by all intents and purposes. So, what's your argument about tattooing me now?" I hopped off the desk and followed Levi to the corner of his office. He was pulling a paper from the printer and gathering other supplies for the client I was sure he prayed would arrive soon. When he turned around, his back to the wall, me at his front, he immediately tensed as he realized he was trapped. Not trapped for real. He could push me out of the way with his pinky, but Levi would never use force against me unless I begged him to—which I wasn't above doing.

"Jay, get out of the way." Levi growled.

"Not until you tell me why you won't tattoo me." I pressed.

"I think you're too young. I'm not sure you really want a tattoo. And, I think you just like the idea of it along with pestering me about it."

I wondered if Levi recognized the weakness of his argument as quickly as I did.

"I think you're afraid to tattoo me." I stepped closer, pressing him against the wall and reveling in the warmth of his bare forearms against my chest. "I think you're scared of what would happen if you got me half naked on your table. You'd have your hands all over my virgin skin, you'd see my body shiver at your touch, and you'd feel the heat between us," I whispered while trailing a finger down his bicep.

"I'm not scared of a damn thing," Levi bit out.

"Then prove it. Tattoo me. Ink your mark deep in my skin." I was as turned on by our little encounter as I hoped Levi was.

The front door bell clanged as someone entered.

I leaned down and placed a tiny, chaste kiss to the inked skin of Levi's arm, which was crossed across his chest. Glancing at him, I thrilled at the brief glimmer of interest in his eyes and the slight flare of his nostrils before I stepped back. "Saved by the bell…this time."

As Levi gripped the papers in one hand and made to exit his office without so much as a look back at me, I reached for his elbow and let my touch trail slowly down his arm until our fingertips brushed together. "But, *this* is going to happen."

The look of pure panic flashing across Levi's face told me he comprehended I was speaking of more than just the tattoo.

"I've got a client. I'll see you at your party." Levi's words were rushed.

"Midnight at BJ's Burgers & Beers before we head to your house after my first legal drink. Don't be late. Last one there has to take a body shot off me. Or maybe I'll do one off the last to arrive." I wagged my brows and prayed Levi would get held up at the shop and be the last to arrive at my party.

Chapter 3

Levi

The last thing I wanted was show up late for Jay's party. Actually, I didn't even want to go, but my friends and cousin wouldn't let me live it down if I missed the kid's birthday. I'd likely have more explaining to do by missing the event than just going and gritting my teeth through the whole thing.

No way in hell could I do a body shot off of Jay after he'd primed and teased me so thoroughly at the shop before my last client.

My client turned out to be a fainter so the appointment took double the amount of time. I could have left the cleanup for later, but I wouldn't be open the rest of the weekend and it wasn't in me to leave a mess. Instruments needed cleaned and disinfected, trash thrown out, and supplies set up for the next appointment.

By the time I'd cleaned the sanitized everything, flew through a shower in the back of the shop, and put on nicer clothes, I knew I'd be the last one to show up. *Fuck.* If I knew Jay, he'd probably coerced the rest of the group to get there super early so I'd be the last one no matter what.

Walking into Cody Parker's family establishment, BJ's Burgers & Beers, I breathed deeply and steeled myself against whatever the night would bring. We could all have a good time without things getting out of control or Jay thinking he'd made any headway with his ridiculous notion of there being an *us*.

"'Bout time you dragged your ass in here." My cousin, Micah, hollered. He sat at a table in the dimly lit bar.

Cody had shut the place down at eleven forty-five so we had the bar to ourselves.

"I made it before midnight."

"Yeah, but we've been drinking since eleven. You need to catch up." Cole laughed.

Glancing around, I saw a very impatient Jay waiting on the clock to strike midnight, a totally buzzed Micah and Cole, Cody sipping a beer, and a very sober Kennedy. I nudged him. "You the DD?"

Kennedy smirked and nodded. "Yeah, someone has to keep these yahoos safe."

"Oh, and you're the one to do it, right *Officer Marks?*" Cody sneered.

"Yeah, I can take care of you…I mean…all of you just fine." Kennedy hooked thumbs in his belt loops and stepped closer to Cody, his chest bumping hard against Cody's crossed arms.

The movement sloshed Cody's beer over the edge of his cup, but neither man seemed to notice.

"Want me to show you how much I can take care of you?" Kennedy's words were low, but those of us not drunk could hear them clearly.

I glanced at Jay and he raised his brows and shrugged.

"Fuck you, Marks." Cody slammed his beer on the bar and stood to his full height to take advantage of the slight difference in their builds. "The day I need or want you taking care of me will be a cold day in hell."

"Better grab a jacket," Kennedy taunted without taking his eyes from Cody.

"Boys, boys, back to your corners." Jay clapped his hands and stepped between Cody and Kennedy, pushing them apart. "You two can have your little leather Daddy love fest some other time." When both men started to protest, Jay shushed them. "Tonight is *my* birthday which means everything is about *me*." He checked the time. "And, we have exactly one minute until I can legally drink. Cody, will you pour us all a drink, please?" Jay rubbed his hands together.

Cody gave Kennedy one last glare before stalking behind the bar and slamming down five shot glasses and a water glass.

Tequila for five, a shaker of salt, and a bowl of lime wedges was produced alongside Kennedy's glass of ice water.

Once the backs of our hands were salted and ready, Jay cleared his throat. "I just wanted to say thanks. I came here lost and alone. Over the past two years, you all have become true friends who I can count on and turn to for anything. I know you'd probably rather be doing something else this weekend, but it makes me happy to know you're willing to spend my birthday with me." Jay held up his glass. "Cheers!"

Glasses clinked, salt was licked, tequila swallowed, and limes sucked before a group *Happy Birthday* was shouted.

"Okay, one more before we head out." Micah poured another shot of tequila into Jay's glass.

Micah wasn't stumbling drunk, but he was definitely buzzed.

"I believe I heard something about the last to arrive had to do a body shot? Jay, it's your birthday, so you get to choose the who and how."

"Micah, shut the fuck up." I growled at my cousin. "Besides, who even *does* body shots anymore?"

Jay hopped up on the bar and pretended to think it over while Micah came over to whisper in my ear. "What's wrong? You say he's not your type at all so it shouldn't be an issue."

Jay pursed his lips and tapped a long thin finger against his beautiful pout. "Hmmm, I think Levi gets to be my subject. Lay down, Daddy. I've never done a body shot off of someone. You get to be my first."

The whole group laughed. I groaned but I wasn't surprised Jay had chosen me.

"Go on, Cousin. He doesn't affect you at all, remember? So, having him lick salt from your stomach and suck a lime from your mouth shouldn't be a problem." Micah's breath tickled at my ear, and I wanted to punch the motherfucker in his drunk-ass face.

"Whatever. Let's get this damn cluster fuck of a party over with." I hoisted myself up to the bar and laid back. When Jay straddled my legs, I blinked as all the blood rushed from my head to my cock. I knew I was going to pass out.

Jay sat all prim and proper on my thighs, his shot glass in one hand and the saltshaker in the other.

Wiggling his perfect ass against me, he smiled seductively. "Lift your shirt."

The way his words rasped against his throat did wicked things to my body. Glad for the dim light of the bar, I willed my cock to behave and lifted my shirt to expose my stomach.

Jay shook the salt and hummed, "Mmmm, I love a good salty treasure trail." Setting the salt aside, Jay grabbed a lime wedge. "Open up, Daddy." Jay leaned forward, close to my face, and placed the lime between my teeth.

The next thirty seconds were my exact definition of heaven and hell.

Jay lowered himself to lick the salt from my stomach, shot back his tequila, and shimmied his long arms and legs up my torso to bite the lime from my teeth.

I longed to pull him back, to devour his mouth, to taste the lime, liquor and Jay, but he was already sliding from the bar.

Offering his hand, Jay pulled me into a sitting position before yanking me to the floor. Leaning close, he stepped between my legs as I tried to gather myself. With his hands behind my neck, Jay tipped my head down to look at him. I expected something outrageous, something saucy, something very Jay. But the kid simply held my gaze for several heartbeats, his chest heaving against mine as I fought to return my breathing to normal.

Blueridge Junction didn't have any nightclubs for dancing, so we headed about thirty minutes east of town to a gay nightclub known for strong, cheap drinks, and good music. Why we were going dancing was beyond me. Micah and Cole would have been wrapped in each other's arms making out no matter where we went, Cody and Kennedy looked as if they'd rather kill each other than dance, and no way in hell was I getting on the dance floor. Especially not with Jay.

"Drinks!" Cole crowed before buying the first round.

I pitied he and Micah their hangovers the next day. We made our way to a tall-top table and pulled up chairs. The club was busy, but manageable.

Cole weaved his way through the crowd with a gorgeous man following. "Gentlemen, *this* is Topher. He was kind enough to help me with the drinks."

Cody and Kennedy nearly drowned in their own drool as they eye-fucked the man.

"Nice to meet you, Topher." Cody never took his eyes from the scantily clad waiter.

"You too." Topher gawked back and forth between Cody and Kennedy. "You fine gentlemen let me know if there's *anything* I can do for you."

"Something tells me he's not just talking about drinks," Jay chirped.

We all snickered, and I caught a look between Cody and Kennedy as Topher left the table. I wasn't nearly buzzed enough to miss it, but I couldn't put my finger on what it meant.

"I bet Topher the Gopher would like to come to Sunday services at the B & B," Micah drawled.

"Mmhm, he looked as if he was begging for an invite, Cody." Cole smiled over his glass. "I bet he'd be ready, willing, and waiting to be your plaything."

"Okay, enough of that." Jay piped up. "Cody and Kennedy can look for their play toys on their own time. Tonight is about *me*." Jay drained his drink as Cody and Kennedy scowled first at him and then at each other.

Micah and Cole laughed, kissed, and then stumbled their way to the dance floor.

"Dance with me, Daddy?" Jay purred in my ear with a light caress to my thigh.

"Nah, I don't really dance." It wasn't a lie. I'd never been a big dancer even in my younger days, and I most certainly hadn't danced since college.

"Suit yourself. But, the invitation is open." Jay slid from his chair and sidled up next to Cody. "Papa Bear? You want to dance? Officer?"

When Cody and Kennedy both declined, Jay shrugged it off. "Fine, I'm going to dance with Papi and the Professor. Join me if you change your mind."

For the next thirty minutes, I downed three shots of fireball and stared daggers at Jay and the men who dared to touch him on the dance floor.

"You know, for someone you supposedly aren't *at all* into, you sure do seem quite fixated on watching the kid dance," Cody groused.

"Yeah, well, for two people who *supposedly* hate each other's guts, you two do a pretty piss-poor job of disguising the fact that you want to fuck each other's brains out and throw ol' Topher in there as a bonus." I shot back at Cody before glaring at Kennedy with a silent dare.

"Maybe you should go dance with him," Kennedy suggested.

As the DD he was probably the most logical voice of reason. "Maybe you should mind your own damn business, Marks." I pushed from the table and stalked to the dance floor.

I knew Jay was putting on a show for me. He was an amazing dancer and he knew it. He'd caught me looking more than once since he'd made his way out to the floor. Well, birthday boy would have to find his fun elsewhere. The show was over.

The three quick shots added to the other alcohol I'd consumed, the writhing lustful heat of swaying bodies mixed with the thump of the bass, and the darkness lit only sporadically by flashes of light all swirled together until I found myself in the middle of the dance floor with a body in front of me and a body behind me.

Without the extra liquor, I would have simply walked away. But, I was warm from the liquor. The music touched me deep inside, and the body pressed against my front was the one I'd been longing to hold for much too long. The atmosphere and the alcohol took over. Swaying to the music, I closed my eyes and joined the mass of bodies thrusting and rocking on the dance floor.

Cole danced behind me. His main focus was Micah grinding against his ass, but Cole stayed at my back to keep me close to Jay. Cole gripped my arms and moved them to Jay's shoulders.

That first touch lit a fire to my already simmering insides, and I jerked Jay closer until his ass was flush with my body. As soon as I made contact with Jay, I melted into his back as he lifted his arms above his head and wrapped them around my neck. Jay's slim body stretched out before me and my hands greedily trailed from his shoulders to his hips and back again as the little minx rubbed his ass against my cock.

Turning in my arms as one song ended and a slower one began, Jay kept his arms wrapped around my neck. "Thought you didn't dance."

Ignoring his question, I held his waist lightly, wanting to grip him against me tightly, but fighting to keep control. "This means nothing." My words were forced through gritted teeth.

"Whatever you say, Daddy, but I think it means a lot more than nothing." Jay thrust his arousal against mine and moaned.

My own groan was involuntary and I hated it. "Why me?" I asked over the thumping beat.

Jay cocked his head to the side. "What?"

"Why me? You could have any and every guy in this place, why come to BJ and set your sights on me?" It was something I'd wondered often since Jay's arrival in town.

He shrugged. "I came for the job. Finding you in BJ was an added bonus."

"But, why not move on when you figured out I wasn't interested?" I didn't want to hurt the kid, but I really needed him to let it go.

"You're gorgeous, you're fun to mess with, and I'm a determined little gay boy. I'm like a dog and you're my bone." Jay teased but then his expression sobered. "And, you're the first person who has ever looked at me as more than a pretty face and sexy body. You make me feel safe and protected. I know *when* we happen it will be the real thing, not just you using me."

No one had ever spoken such words to me. Of course I'd never use the kid, and I'd keep him safe. As much as my head said I should tell Jay once again that *nothing* would happen between us, my heart whispered to let it go for a while. For tonight only, my heart won the battle, and I wrapped Jay in a hug and let him sway in my arms until the song was over.

By the time Kennedy poured Micah and Cole into the vehicle, my buzz had settled to a dull roar. Cody had nursed the same beer for most of the night. And Jay's youthfulness, dancing, and fast metabolism had helped to wear off the alcohol quite quickly. With the six of us loaded in the truck, Kennedy headed toward BJ.

"Oh, let's get food!" Jay clapped.

Micah and Cole groaned and held onto each other, but Cody, Kennedy, and I all glanced at around and nodded. Food actually sounded good.

"Let's get it to go. I don't think taking those two lushes anywhere would be the greatest idea." Cody shot a thumb over his shoulder toward Micah and Cole.

I called in an order that could have fed a football team. Cheeseburgers, pancakes, French toast, bacon, tater tots, and homemade donuts. I knew we wouldn't eat it all, but the thought of Jay being hungry did weird things to my insides.

Forty-five minutes later, we were pulling in at my house with five to-go bags of food.

"Micah, Cole, come on. We're home. You two need to puke, drink a ton of water, and take some aspirin or your hangover is going to have a hangover." Cody dragged the two men from the truck. "Stay out here and see if you can throw up."

Micah and Cole groaned in unison. I had a feeling they'd be able to meet that goal pretty quickly.

Walking inside, I flipped on the lights and was immediately bombarded with pink. "Oh my god, it's like a flamingo barfed all over my house."

"Do you like it?" Jay bounced up and down.

"It's very pink. Very loud. Very Jay." I had no other words as I took in the absolute plethora of pink beads, pink streamers, pink confetti, pink balloons, and pink table décor.

"Thank you, kind sir." Jay gave a mock bow and moved to the kitchen like a bird honing in on its prey.

Digging into the bags of food, Jay pulled out all of the containers and the four of us crowded around to fill plates.

The door opened and Micah and Cole stumbled into the kitchen.

"Feel any better boys?" I asked.

"Little. Got rid of most of the alcohol. Can we eat then go sleep in our own bed? We'll come back in the morning." Micah started plating food for himself and handed Cole a plate.

"Well, it's already morning, but sure that can be allowed," Jay proclaimed. "But, no excuses. Once you are awake, you are back here to celebrate with me."

Micah and Cole nodded and trudged toward the door with their food. The men were still living in my guesthouse while their own home was being built on Blueridge Hill.

"Drink a bottle or two of water and Gatorade before bed. Take some aspirin." Kennedy advised as he walked them to the door.

"And don't forget my gift!" Jay shouted at their retreating backs.

We all laughed and moved to the living room to stuff our faces. By four o'clock in the morning, we were stuffed and sleepy.

"I'm going to bed. You're all welcome to crash wherever you want," I paused and looked at Jay, "*not* in my bed though."

Jay wrinkled his nose.

"You know where the blankets are. We'll clean up and get the day started once we get some sleep. We shouldn't sleep past noon." I glanced at Cody and Kennedy as they shucked their shoes and stretched out on the two couches. They were likely asleep before Jay and I even left the room.

"You think they need blankets?" I hesitated at the living room doorway.

"Nah, they're out cold." Jay shook his head. "If they wake cold maybe they can warm each other up." He waggled his brows in the dimly lit hallway.

"Yeah, there's definitely *something* between them. More than just hating each other."

"I think this is one of those times where hate and love are very closely related. Those two are so hot for each other they could light this place on fire if they'd ever give in and let it happen." Jay paused at the guest room's door.

"Two strong personalities like Cody and Kennedy are bound to fight, but I think they could be good together." I spoke my thoughts aloud. "You want to shower?"

Jay's eyes were sleepy, but he nodded and grinned. "With you?"

"No," I grumbled. I grabbed him a towel and a bar of soap although I knew he could have found them himself. "Sleep tight." I fought the overwhelming urge to gather the kid in my arms and kiss the top of his head.

"G'night." Jay mumbled as he closed the bathroom door.

Moments later I heard the shower turn on so I headed toward my own room and my own shower. As I was crawling into bed ten minutes later, I heard a loud thump down the hallway. Jay's whispered curse drew me from bed and out the door.

Flipping on the hallway light, I squinted against the brightness and saw Jay doubled over holding his elbow. "What happened?"

"Sorry, didn't mean to wake you." Jay grimaced as he rubbed his elbow. "I didn't want to turn on the light. I banged my elbow on the doorframe. Totally my own fault."

"Don't worry about turning on the light. I wasn't even in bed yet." I turned on the bedside lamp in the guest room. "Come on, let's get you safely in bed before you injure yourself more." I patted the bed.

Jay flipped off the hallway light and smiled sleepily as he made his way to the bed. His lean torso begged for my touch, my lips, and I forced my mind not to picture what was or wasn't under his pajama pants.

"You going to tuck me in, Daddy?" Jay smirked as he tumbled to the bed and climbed under the covers.

"Don't push your luck, birthday boy." I shook my head and headed toward the door even though my entire body screamed to slide under the covers and pull him close. Had I ever in my life wanted to kiss a man as badly as I wanted to kiss Jay Owens? Pulling the door shut behind me with a little more force than necessary, I rolled my eyes at the saucy little chuckle that sounded from the other side and marched to my room.

Hoping the exhaustion, alcohol, and food would bring quick sleep, I climbed into bed and prayed for a dreamless night.

"Rise and shine!" Jay chirped from the doorway of my room. "Micah and Cole are among the living and on their way over. You need to get your gorgeous ass out of bed and start some coffee while I go wake Papa Bear and Officer Bear."

I groaned in acknowledgment of Jay's wakeup call and pulled the covers over my head.

By the time I heard Micah and Cole coming through the backdoor, I had brushed my teeth, washed my face, and felt somewhat human. At least the kid had let us sleep until eleven forty-five. Jay was like a kid on Christmas morning. Only he wasn't a kid, it wasn't Christmas, and it was only officially morning for a few more minutes.

"Mimosas!" Jay crowed as he emerged from the kitchen through the damn ridiculous beads with a tray of champagne flutes.

The five of us sat sprawled across my living room on couches and recliner and a love seat and stared at him.

"Is he serious right now?" Kennedy seemed to voice his question to no one in particular.

"I never kid about mimosas," Jay deadpanned before breaking into a breathtaking smile. "Now, everyone grab a glass. It's time to toast the birthday boy."

"You're making us toast you?" I couldn't help but laugh. "Of course you are." I shook my head.

"I toasted all of you last night. It's only proper you return the favor on this, my day of birth."

Jay's haughty words were delivered without so much as a crack in his serious face. But, a split second later he was rolling on the couch laughing his ass off.

"Toast me bitches!" He grabbed his own glass and waited with his glass raised and an arched brow.

Micah cleared his throat. "Cole and I will go first." He picked up his glass.

The rest of us followed suit.

"Happy birthday to a guy who can always be counted on to bring a laugh. And who will tell you like it is, even if it's not easy."

"Happy birthday to Jay. Thank you for being there for Micah and me when we were both too dumb to fix things ourselves." Cole smiled.

Kennedy chuckled before speaking. "Happy birthday, Jay. You bring a special light to this sometimes sleepy backward little town."

"To Jay," Cody's words were gruff from emotion or sleep or both. "Thank you for keeping me in business with your appetite."

Everyone smiled. Cody gave Jay more food than what the kid purchased.

Five pairs of eyes turned toward me. My chest tightened, my pulse sped up, and I swallowed a lump in my throat before rushing the words from my mouth. "Happy birthday to a guy who keeps me on my toes."

"Cheers!" We all clinked glasses and drank to Jay.

"Presents!" Jay rushed from the room and returned with five small gift bags. "You guys get gifts first." He handed us each a personalized bag.

"You got us gifts for *your* birthday?" Cody peeked inside the bag.

"Yep! It's not much, but I picked the gifts out for you each specifically. Now, open them." Jay bounced on the couch like a little kid.

I wished my phone was close enough to record the hilarity of the moment. Five grown men dug into dainty little gift bags and pulled out a jock strap of a different color and design. Glancing around at each other and seeing that we'd all gotten the same gift with slight variations, we burst out laughing.

"You got us all jock straps?" Micah fell onto Cole's lap in a fit of laughter.

"Yes, jock straps can make a man feel very sexy. I wanted you all to feel good. Maybe we can each wear them for that special someone..." Jay batted his eyelashes at me.

Cody and Kennedy stared at each other and then at the jocks before grunting and shoving them back into the bags.

"Thanks, Jay. Very nice." Cody's words were clipped.

"Now, I believe it's time for *my* gifts." Jay clapped his hands together.

Kid was so damn cute in his excitement. I was fuckin' screwed.

CHAPTER 4

JAY

I absolutely adored the looks on my friends'
faces when they discovered their handpicked jock
straps. I knew Micah and Cole would be wearing
them soon, Cody and Kennedy would deny that they
imagined the other in the jock, and, if my dreams
came true, I'd see Levi in his sooner rather than later.

"I gotta ask," Cody began, "did we all get the
same lists?"

"No, I personalized them for each of you." I
smiled innocently. "Why?"

Cody laughed and shook his head. "Just
wondering."

My friends all produced gift bags or envelopes,
and I stood in the middle of the room. "Okay, Micah
and Cole, I asked you for sexy, nerdy teacher glasses,
a paddle, sex on the hood of a car in the shop, and a

pair of those coveralls." I read through the list I'd provided. "Hand it over."

Inside the bag was a six-pack of really nice beer, a sweet red wine, a gift certificate to a movie theater the next town over, and a week of meals at BJ's Burgers & Beers. "Awww, you guys, this is all so sweet. Even though you deterred from the list— which is never recommended by the way—you did a great job and got me things I love and I'll use." I rushed to give them both big hugs. "Thank you so much."

"Next up is Cody." I turned toward Papa Bear as I pulled a copy of his list from my pocket. "I asked you for a ball gag, a whip, and a harness." I gestured at him to hand over a gigantic gift bag. Digging in, I discovered a beautiful wine rack and a week's worth of meals at BJ's Burgers & Beers. "Simply beautiful, both the rack and the meals. Thank you so very much." I walked to Cody and pulled him into a hug. "But, I'm not forgetting about that harness and ball gag." I meant for the whole group to hear my dramatic whisper and joined in with their laughter.

"Okay, Kennedy, you're next." I scanned the list and smirked. "Handcuffs, a gun belt, and a cop hat. Easy enough for my Officer Bear." Kennedy handed me an envelope. Inspecting the contents, I found another week's worth of meals already paid for at the B & B plus a yearlong subscription to a wine of the month club. My mouth formed a little O. "Look at my Papa Bear and Officer Bear working together to give me the gift of wine." I winked at them both before wrapping Kennedy in a huge hug.

"And now, it's Daddy's turn." I pinned my gaze on Levi and watched him squirm. "I asked for butt plugs, condoms, a blind fold, and new jocks." Swaying my hips as I approached him, I put my hands on his shoulders and ignored the uninterested message his crossed arms were sending. "Things I thought would be all sorts of fun to play with."

Levi rolled his eyes, grunted, and reached for his back pocket. Producing two envelopes, he handed them to me. "Open the one on top first. It's useful but pretty boring."

A nervous excitement ran through me as I opened the first envelope.

"Another week of meals completely paid for at the B & B. Thank you all so much for this. Being able to eat so well and save my cash for a whole month will be super helpful in getting some savings put aside." The gift was beyond useful and meant a lot to know they thought about my well-being. Sliding my finger under the flap of the second envelope, I took a moment to read what the gift certificate said. Slapping a hand to my mouth, I muffled an ecstatic scream. "I swear to god, bitch! If this is a joke I'm never forgiving you!"

Levi smiled his gorgeous easy smile and shook his head. "No joke. It's for real."

Staring at the words on the gift certificate, I felt my eyes blur with tears.

"What is it?" Micah prompted.

"A tattoo. Anything I want." My hand trembled at my lips. "Thank you so much, Levi."

"Whoa, you got him to say your actual name. Must be magic," Cole teased.

"Nice going, dude. Glad you got to go last. None of our gifts could have lived up to that," Cody groused. "Aww, look at the kid. It's like he just saw all of his dreams come true."

I smiled through the tears. "Not *all* of them, but this gift means so very much. Thank you." I launched myself at Levi and let him wrap his warm strong arms around me. "Seriously, thank you," I whispered for only Levi to hear.

"So, what tattoo do you want?" Kennedy inadvertently broke the brief moment Levi and I were sharing.

I took a deep breath and enjoyed the last few seconds of connection Levi and I had before he let me go. Pausing for a moment, I thought about the question. "I have no clue."

The whole group laughed.

"You've been begging for a tattoo for two years. How do you not know what you want?" Micah pulled Cole into his arms and kissed the side of his head as he spoke to me.

I shook my head to clear the happy fog. "I don't know. I think I was so focused on pestering and begging and irritating Levi that I never really gave much thought to what I'd get if he ever gave in and said yes."

"Well, you better figure something out." Cody smirked.

Turning to Levi, I suddenly felt shy. "Can you design something? Just for me? A Levi Wells original you'll never put on another person's body for as long as you live?"

Levi stared at me for a moment. "Gee, no pressure or anything."

His gaze scanned my body, and my blood went from the usual simmer around Levi to a slow, rolling boil.

"Yeah, I've got some ideas."

"Whatever you design will be perfect. I want it inked on me before I see it." I trusted Levi completely and knew whatever he created would be exquisite.

"You don't even want to approve the design?" Levi cocked a brow.

"No, I trust you. You're the artist, you're the professional. My body is yours to do with what you wish." I winked and totally meant the innuendo exactly the way it sounded.

Levi's dark stare bored into me for several moments before he nodded. "Deal." His large hand reached out and gripped mine and a tremor of electricity traveled between us. "I'll get the design ready and then we'll get to work."

Forgetting every other person in the room, I kept my hand in Levi's and stepped closer. "I look forward to it. More than you know."

~*~*~

We spent the afternoon snoozing, watching movies, and generally resting from the night before. I caught Levi staring at me more than once, and my heart belly flopped each time his dark gaze met mine. By evening, I was itching to get the party started again. Drinks, pizza, and cupcakes were on the agenda.

"I can't believe you really want to spend your birthday night around a bonfire." Frowning, Cody helped stack the wood and get the fire started.

"What? I'm not your typical gay." I popped a hip and crossed my arms over my chest.

The rest of the guys threw their heads back in laughter.

"You're like the most stereotypical gay in so many ways, but then you go and ask for a bonfire, pizza, and cupcakes for your birthday and blow the stereotypes out of the water." Micah slapped me on the back.

"What can I say? I like to keep people guessing." I saw nothing wrong celebrating my birthday with a bonfire on a beautiful hill.

The grumble of a truck engine announced the arrival of Hank Parker with the pizzas. "Do I get a delivery tip?" he joked as he climbed from the truck and brought the pizzas to the back of Levi's house.

"Nope, you took longer than thirty minutes, so the pizzas are free and no tip for you." Cody teased his dad. "Seriously though, thanks for picking the pizzas up."

"No problem at all." Hank turned from his son and smiled at me. "Happy birthday, Jay. Marian and Susan should be along shortly with the cupcakes. They were delighted with your request and have spent all day baking and decorating."

I couldn't help but clasp my hands together in excitement. At that exact moment, Marian's car could be heard on the driveway and Hank went to the front to help with the cupcake delivery.

Three tiered cupcake displays were placed on the picnic table and I nearly stopped breathing. Before me were the most delectable, delicate, divine confectionary pieces of art I'd ever seen. Each cupcake had been hand decorated and was slightly different from its neighboring delicacy. Crystals of sugar sparkled in the early evening sunset. My mouth watered at the thought of consuming the treats, but my heart didn't want their beauty disturbed.

"These are the most gorgeous cupcakes I've ever seen in my entire life," I gushed as I rushed at Marian and Susan and hugged them both. "Thank you so very much. No one has ever made me a birthday cake, so these mean more than you'll ever know."

"You're so very welcome. We had a ball baking and decorating." Marian kissed my cheek.

"I don't know that I've ever had so much fun making cupcakes, so thank *you*." Susan returned my hug.

By the time the parental figures said their goodbyes I was starving. Levi set up another table and chairs as Cody and Kennedy worked with the fire. Settling in with beer and pizza, I glanced around at my circle of friends and felt my heart warm.

"So is it everything you'd hoped your birthday would be?" Cole asked around a mouthful of pizza.

"Honestly, you guys will think I'm being sappy or overly dramatic, but it's truly the best birthday party I've ever had." My words caught on an unexpected lump in my throat.

"How's that?" Micah cocked his head.

"I wasn't lying when I said no one had ever made me a birthday cake. I think I got myself a tiny store bought one when I was about thirteen." Wiping my mouth on my napkin, I figured in for a penny in for a pound. "Growing up, my home life pretty much sucked. So, having food to eat, cupcakes baked just for me, and five men I consider to be real friends helping to celebrate is pretty damn great."

"Why did home life suck?" Levi's voice was gruff.

I took another bite of pizza and chewed it slowly while thinking about his question. Three swigs of beer later, I took a deep breath and the words unfurled from my mouth. "My dad left when I was a baby. My mom was, *is*, a complete alcoholic and drug addict. I mean, she's fairly functional and she's addicted to prescription pills, but she's still an addict. She missed school plays, parent teacher conferences, and bake sales. But, she also forgot to buy groceries and only made dinners when she was feeling guilty. Sometimes she'd come off a bender and feel so guilty that she'd cook two or three nights in a row. But, mostly, I was on my own." I shifted in my seat at the ugly memories. "It was really bad when I was little. I have no clue how she took care of me when I was a baby. I probably got my spunkiness and tenacity from surviving that time period. From my earliest memories, Mom would leave a box of cereal where I could reach it. If we had milk and bread, I was feeling lucky. I learned quickly to load up on food at breakfast and lunch when I was at school." I took a look around at the guys and realized they were hanging on my every word. The fire crackled and popped in the silence.

"Now, don't go feeling sorry for me. I'm a survivor. Everything got harder as I got older and figured out I liked boys. I was better able to fend for myself as far as food, but the emotional chaos of middle school and high school for a scrawny, neglected, gay kid was pure and total hell." Swigging the last of my beer and popping another one open, I went on. "So, I got the heck out of that town as quickly as I could and ended up here. I've always loved to dance, and I've always been really good at it. When I saw the ad for Strip Teaze, I figured I had nothing to lose." I smiled self-consciously at the guys. "And, that, my dear friends is the story of Jay Owens. But, you know what? I'm okay with it because it made me who I am today and it brought me to Blueridge Junction. And maybe, just maybe, someday I'll get to be an official BJ Boy like the rest of you." I kicked into my normal humorous banter to both ease the tension and take all the attention off of the sob story I'd just poured out.

Breaking the silence, I stood and walked with my empty plate and beer can to the large trashcan Levi had pulled from the garage. I felt his presence before he even spoke. His voice a low growl at my ear.

"Never again."

His words were a promise. "Huh?" I turned to face him.

"I don't want to ever again hear about you being hungry or without something. If it ever comes to that, you tell us. If I find out you've gone hungry or went without a necessity and haven't told us, I'll bend you over my knee and spank your ass so hard you won't be able to sit down for a week." Levi roughly grabbed the back of my head and pulled me forward so his lips could plant a hard kiss to my forehead. "And it won't be a fun type of spanking. You hear me?"

My whimper and feeble nod would have to suffice because no way was I able to produce words at that moment.

"Good." Levi let me go. "Let's go play whatever damn drinking game you've got planned."

I walked in stunned silence back toward the fire and plopped down in my chair. I'd been telling myself something existed between Levi and me for two years. And I'd always believed it. But, that night, my belief took on a whole new level. No matter how I looked at it, Levi Wells cared about me. My heart sang hallelujah as I prepared to explain the drinking game's rules to my friends.

All the guys, except Levi, hid smirks and raised eyebrows behind their beer and pizza while I gathered my wits. Levi pretended nothing monumental had taken place between us. However, my heart and the faces of the four other men around the bonfire proved that something big had definitely transpired.

Shaking my head to clear the glittery fog of sheer elation from my brain, I simply smiled at them all, winked, and blew a kiss. "Okay, gentlemen, the game is called 'Never Have I Ever' and it goes like this." I interlocked my fingers and stretched my arms to crack my knuckles before grabbing a new beer. The liquor warmed me and giddiness rippled under my skin. "Player one says something they've never done. If any other player *has* done the activity, they have to drink. If no one else has done the activity then player one has to drink. Here's an example: Never have I ever been snorkeling." I watched around the circle to see who would drink.

Kennedy raised his beer and took a drink.

"Nice. Where did you snorkel?" Micah asked.

"On a trip to Florida in high school. Saw some awesome schools of fish and a pod of dolphins swam up and played for a little bit."

"Any sharks?" Cole inquired.

"Only little ones about the size of my forearm." Kennedy turned his gaze to me. "So, is it my turn?"

I nodded and prepared to learn about my friends and get a good buzz at the same time.

Kennedy tapped his bottom lip for a moment. "Never have I ever had sex in an airplane."

Everyone glanced at each other.

"Damn, we're a boring bunch." Kennedy laughed as he took another drink. "Okay, who's turn now?"

"Just move clockwise." I pointed toward Cody.

Cody narrowed his eyes at the group.

The fire cast orange and black shadows on our faces and the pungent smoke billowed into the night sky.

"Never have I ever had a threesome."

Kennedy almost gave himself whiplash turning to look at Cody. The sexual tension between the two was palpable on a normal day, but skyrocketed with Cody's statement.

Suspicious looks were cast around the group until finally Micah chuckled and took a drink.

Cole gawked at him. "You and I can discuss *that* later, mister."

Micah leaned over the arm of his chair to kiss Cole's proffered pucker. "In detail. I promise." Micah straightened in his seat. "Never have I ever kissed a girl."

Kennedy, Cole, Cody, and I all took a drink while Levi's smug mug observed.

"Do tell," Micah prodded.

"I was in Kindergarten so maybe the kiss doesn't count. And, technically, *she* kissed me." Cole shrugged.

Kennedy took another drink as if bolstering himself to tell a story. "I was actually engaged to a woman."

"You're bi?" Cody jumped in.

"No, I was convinced in my younger days it would be easier to hide myself. She was a great girl, a true friend. But, I chickened out before the wedding, couldn't follow through. I didn't want to put her through a divorce later on down the road. I finally admitted that losing my friends and family was a risk I'd have to take, because I couldn't face a life of pretending to be someone I wasn't." He finished his beer. "Last I heard, Racheal was married to a fireman and they have five kids. She seemed happy the last time I saw her. I've never regretted ending things, but I do regret any pain I put her through while trying to figure out myself."

I sat quietly for a moment before turning my attention toward Cody.

"Mine isn't nearly as dramatic. I was at a party in sixth grade. They were playing some version of Spin the Bottle or something like that. Betsy Roth spun the bottle and it landed on me. She leaned over and kissed me smack on the lips before I could even sputter a protest." Cody shook his head at the memory.

"Betsy Roth? Did her parents hate the poor girl? That's an unfortunate name." I giggled. "I bet she got all kinds of shit about the flag." Knowing I had reached buzzed, and was headed toward drunk very quickly, I took another drink and hiccupped. "Shit, whose turn is it?"

"I'll go." Cole raised his hand like a student.

"The floor is yours, Professor," I teased.

"Never have I ever had sex on a train." Cole watched the group expectantly and laughed out loud when Micah, Levi, and Cody all took a drink.

"What?" Levi shrugged. "We grew up in a railroad town. I think almost every native to Blueridge Junction has had sex on a train. I'd say at least a quarter of the town was probably *conceived* on a train." He popped a new beer open. "Okay, my turn." He glanced at me briefly before speaking. "Never have I ever had sex with someone more than ten years younger than me."

Cody snorted and Micah almost fell out of his chair laughing.

"Gee, that's fairly specific." Cole smirked.

None of us drank so Levi had to take a drink. His glassy eyes smoldered as hot as the nearby flames as he watched me over the beer can. "Your turn."

Feeling off-kilter from Levi's words, I stood from my camp chair, swaying slightly as I tried to steady myself. With my beer raised in the air, I hummed a little song before blurting the first thing that came to my mind. "Never have I ever had sex."

The stunned silence was deafening. Only the popping and hissing of the fire filled the air as all five pairs of eyes were glued to me in utter shock. Well, four pairs were in utter shock. Cole just shook his head and looked surprised that I'd let out my secret.

Immediately realizing that I'd forgotten to keep my cards close to my chest, I grimaced. "Ooops." I drained the rest of my beer. "So, who wants cupcakes? I think it's time for cupcakes!" I forced a smile and retreated from the fire to seek my tiny gorgeous confections.

I knew Levi was behind me from the moment I left the fire's glowing ring of light. Reaching the cupcakes, I pretended to busy myself with finding plates and napkins.

He pressed up behind me. "Were you telling the truth or was that a drunken glitch?"

Levi's growly words sent shivers down my spine and my cock took immediate interest. Laying my head back against his chest and turning to nuzzle under his chin, I whispered. "Does it matter? Would one way or the other give me more of a chance with you?" I closed my eyes, savoring the warmth of Levi's body against mine.

"Damn it, Jay. Yes it matters." Levi tilted his head until his face was nose-to-nose with mine. "I already can't get you the fuck out of my head. And I *need* you out." He took a deep breath, shuddering as his hands reached around our bodies to capture my hands in his. "Every single part of my head tells me anything between us would be wrong. Even more so now because I know you've never been with a man.

But, my heart hurts every time I think of someone else touching you. Knowing someone else will be your first kills me. My body wants to say *fuck it* and give in to whatever damned crazy feelings are between us. But then my damn brain kicks back in and says I can't."

"Why?" My words were more whine than question.

"How would it look? I own a business. I'm an upstanding member of the community. I can't give in to whatever this is and make people question my morals and decision making." Levi took a step back from me. "I just can't."

I whirled on him, dizzy from the alcohol and the quick movement. "You know what? That's an absolute shit excuse." I poked my finger against Levi's chest. "You're right, you're a business owner and member of this community, but you're hiding behind those things and you're using the town as your own personal beard."

"Everyone in town knows I'm gay." Levi protested.

"No, I mean you're making it sound like you can't be with me because the town will judge you. I say *fuck that*. You're tattooed from head to toe. You're openly gay. Your best friend has weekly leather club meetings at his bar. Your cousin is in a same-sex relationship with a local high school teacher. Based on that, you haven't given a damn what people think about you in a very long time." I crossed both arms over my chest. "But, you sure don't mind pinning the blame on an imaginary fear of what people would think of you." I clenched my teeth to fight the tears that threatened. "And I think that really sucks." I turned and picked up the tower of cupcakes. "Get back to me when you find your fucking balls again." Stomping away from Levi, I approached the fire and four friends who were quiet and wouldn't meet my gaze, as if they hadn't heard every single word.

CHAPTER 5

LEVI

Stalking toward the house, I fought to get my breathing under control. The kitchen was dimly lit, and I leaned against the counter, looking out the window toward the bonfire. My heart and body and mind were in a heated standoff as I watched Jay return to the fire and our friends.

"Hey," Micah spoke from the darkened doorway.

I didn't turn toward my cousin, but I knew he moved further into the room.

"He's right, you know." Micah slapped a hand on my shoulder.

"The fuck he is. He's a horny kid who fancies himself in love with an older man. He knows nothing," I growled and pounded my hands on the sink.

"Keep telling yourself that and you may miss out on something really great." Micah's words hung in the air.

"And what if it hurts?" I whispered.

"Who are you worried about hurting?" Micah leaned against the counter next to me.

"It's not like I want to get hurt, but I'm mostly worried about hurting him." I shrugged not really wanting to put too much thought into my feelings at that moment.

But Micah persisted. "Hurting him how? Emotionally or physically?"

"Both!" I sputtered. "Look at him." I gestured out the window. "He's so damn innocent and fragile. He's barely lived life. I could break him in two both emotionally and physically." My heart raced as I thought about holding Jay's lithe body in arms. My body longed to show him gentle pleasure.

Reading my mind, Micah spoke up. "You'd never hurt him physically."

I was silent for a while then turned to meet my cousin's gaze. "But, what if there's too much different between us? What if we don't work out and it crushes him. Or me?" I let deep down fears come out in my words.

"You've been living on your own, tackling the struggles of losing your parents, taking on the world as an artist, and living as a proud gay man. You're a courageous motherfucker." Micah cocked his head. "I didn't think I'd ever see you afraid of taking a risk."

"It's just scary to think about the pain if it doesn't work out." My words were gravely. Casual hookups in the past meant strings, no emotions, and no pain when we went our separate ways. I liked it that way.

"Yeah, but think of how much love and joy you could have if it *does* work out." Micah's simple words stayed with me as he headed toward the door. "Come on, Jay is passing out cupcakes and I'm not missing it."

"I'll be there in a minute." I didn't turn away from the window as I watched Jay choosing cupcakes and presenting the dessert to each of his friends.

An ache filled my head and heart as I thought of what Jay was choosing to present to me. His body, his heart, his whole self. Who was I to deserve such a thing? Just some small-town artist who would likely never leave BJ. "He needs someone so much better than me." I spoke to the darkness but when I heard the floor creak behind me, I whipped around.

Jay.

"I need you." Gaze direct, Jay stepped toward me. "I tease about the whole Daddy thing, but in some ways it's so very true. I need you to teach me, to guide me, to show me what a relationship can be. I'm not just talking sex either, although I want you to teach me all about that, too." He offered his hand. "But I want you to come to me because your heart wants it, not because I coerce you."

I took his hand in mine and traced a thumb over his smooth, porcelain skin. "I can't make any promises. Can I have some time?"

Jay looked up at me and smiled. "I've been waiting two years. I can wait a while longer." He stepped forward and then rose on his toes to brush a kiss across my cheek. "But, do me a favor?"

I nodded while attempting to not swallow my tongue.

"I know part of you keeps telling you to fight it. To fight against what you're feeling, fight against what we could possibly be to each other, but..." Jay reached up with his other hand to cup my cheek. "Maybe let go enough to see what would happen if you stopped fighting. I promise I won't break. I'd like the chance to prove it to you." He turned toward the door but stopped and looked over his shoulder. "Come back to the party. The cupcakes are amazing."

I smiled at his retreating form and touched my cheek where his precious lips had burned my skin.

Was I willing to let Jay's light into my life? I wasn't convinced our lives fit together. But, I was starting to believe I didn't want a life without Jay in it.

I wadded another piece of paper and tossed it at the pile of wadded balls that littered the floor around my shop's desk. I'd been working on Jay's tattoo design for two weeks. Two long-ass weeks of dreaming about the kid, attempting to ignore his flirting, fighting the longing to pull him into my arms and kiss him senseless, and wracking my brain over the perfect design to permanently ink into his delicate skin.

My mind had shadowy ideas and images of what I wanted to draw, but I couldn't piece them all together. I needed something that represented Jay's beauty, his fragility, his strength. The kid had spun a fabulous web of longing around my feelings and sat as patiently as a spider waiting for me to get snared.

Fuck.

A spider web.

Perfect.

I immediately grabbed a new sheet of paper and began sketching a design before it disappeared from my mind. Twenty minutes later, I had a rough outline of a spider web. The ink would be black, white, and gray with shadows and shading to portray the glistening sparkle of silk in the morning sun. Silvery beads of dew would decorate one portion of the web as the light of an unseen sun shone on the strong yet fragile strands.

Fragile strength. The text would grace the web in an almost camouflaged design that would only be seen by the most perceptive observers.

The design would take up most of Jay's back. Shadows and shading, soft lines and hard lines, the tattoo would be a paradox just like Jay's fragile strength. Just like his out and loud personality and his softer more vulnerable side.

My hands itched to start working. But, I needed to touch up the design before it was ready to place on Jay's body forever.

As if my thoughts summoned him, I straightened as the door of the shop swung open and the angel himself walked in.

"Hiya, Daddy Dearest." Jay smiled and slurped suggestively at the lollipop in his mouth.

"Aren't you a little old for suckers?" I teased.

"Nah, you're never too old for a Blow Pop. I love Blow Pops. Makes me think of blowing Pops. Pops as in Daddy. Blow job for Daddy." Jay popped the candy back in his mouth before slowly pulling it from his lips with a loud pop and then winking before licking the tantalizing red stickiness from his mouth.

Rolling my eyes, I waved the paper in his direction. "I've got the basic bones of your tattoo ready."

Jay clapped. "When can we start?"

My heart did flip-flops at the sparkle in his eye. "What's your work schedule look like? I can probably fit you in for two or three sessions over the next few weeks." I thought through appointments already set up.

"Can't we do it all at once?" Jay pouted.

"Yeah, we could. But, it's probably better to do it in at least two sessions." I'd get the main outline done first and fill in the finer points, shadows, and shading in the second session.

Jay shrugged. "I'm off work for the week, so I can come in anytime that works for you."

"You're off for a week?" Suspicion and worry immediately trickled in. "Why?"

"No big deal. Just a customer got a little handsy during a couple shows and then I started getting some weird calls where the person would just breathe and hang up."

Jay was trying to pull off nonchalant, but I wasn't fooled.

"Chuck told me to take the week off, with pay, and see if things would die down."

"Did he call the police?" I immediately wanted to call Kennedy. "Giving you the week off with pay is nice, but the authorities should know if someone is messing with you. Plus, if a guy got handsy, the police should be looking into that person right away."

"Nah, the handsy guy is a regular. He's from out of town. He and his partner used to come watch the shows, but they broke up recently. I think he's been drinking too much the last couple times he's been in. I don't think he's dangerous, just sad and lonely and unsure of what's next." Jay wandered over and sat on the couch in my office.

"What about the calls? The police could be tracing those." I stood from my desk, leaving the design behind, my mind on other things.

"First," Jay chuckled, "this isn't some police detective show. Second, I've called the numbers back and so has Chuck. The calls come from different numbers each time. When we call them back, they automatically come up as disconnected.

Whoever it is must be calling from different prepaid phones each time."

I walked to the couch and sat at the end so I could turn and face Jay. "I need you to tell Kennedy about all of this."

"It's really not that big of a deal," Jay protested. "I'm just glad to have the week off. I mean, I love to dance, but a week to relax sounds fabulous."

"Nuh-uh, you don't get to pretend like this is nothing." I reached over and grabbed his chin, making him look at me. "Seriously, you either tell Kennedy or I tell him. And no tattoo until he knows."

"Geesh, I call you Daddy but you don't have to actually act like a parent," Jay snapped. "Fine, I'll tell Kennedy. But, you're not playing fair."

"I own the shop, the design, the ink, and the machines. I don't have to play fair." I shrugged. "Maybe you should stay somewhere other than your apartment?"

"No, I'm not packing up and moving because of a couple phone calls. Plus, where would I stay?

With you?" Jay raised his brows. "As much as I would *love* to move in with you, I plan on that happening after you profess your undying love and lust for me. Not because you think I'm some pansy-ass dancer who can't stay alone because of a few heavy breathing phone call hang ups." Jay shot up from the couch, crossed his arms, and stared down at me.

Standing, as well, I laid a hand on his shoulder. "Calm down. It was just a suggestion. I don't want you in danger. If Kennedy agrees it's okay for you to stay at your apartment, I'll drop the subject."

Jay rolled his eyes and huffed. "Fine." He walked to the door. "Well, are you coming or not?"

"Where?" Keeping up with the kid was a full-time job sometimes.

"To tell Kennedy about my heavy breather."

A disbelieving look accompanied Jay's exasperated words.

"Then, we're figuring out the tattoo sessions."

I checked my watch. I had several hours before my next appointment. So I grabbed my keys and locked up the shop before following Jay the few blocks to the police department.

"You can take me to B & B for dinner." Jay winked and hooked his arm in mine as he laughed at the look I gave him.

Fighting Jay's pull was getting harder and harder, so I had to wonder why I was trying to fight it.

Chapter 6

Jay

With Levi at my side, I sat in Kennedy's office at the police department.

"So, will you tell my *father* again that it's okay for me to stay at my own place and that some heavy breather is *not* worth getting his sexy panties in a bunch?" My question was directed at Kennedy, but my message was for Levi. "However, I must say the thought of Levi in sexy panties is beyond hot."

"Damn it, Jay. Knock it off," Levi growled before turning to Kennedy. "There's nothing that can be done? And he's fine to stay by himself?"

Kennedy finished writing some notes before meeting my gaze. "I want you to contact me the moment you feel anything is weird or strange or something feels off. Make note of the numbers calling you, the time the calls come in, if you can hear any background sounds, and if the caller says anything. And you call me immediately when they happen."

Kennedy's words were serious.

He glanced at Levi before speaking. "While it *may* be better to stay somewhere else, I'll say it's likely okay to be at your apartment. For now. If the calls increase or get more threatening, or if anything happens to indicate the stalker knows where you live, then you'll stay elsewhere." Kennedy bit back a smirk. "You're welcome to stay with me for as long as necessary."

"That won't be necessary." Levi bit out. "He can stay with me. I have a lot more room than you do."

I smiled. "Boys, boys. No need to fight. There's plenty of this fabulousness to go around as long as you're willing to share."

Levi popped up from his chair like a jack-in-the-box. "Come on. Let's go."

"Wait, where are we going?" I pretended as if I had no clue how irritated Levi was. "I mean, if you're worried that sharing me with Kennedy will bother Cody we can make it a foursome instead."

Kennedy snorted behind his desk. "Stop messing with the man."

"But it's so fun." I winked before following Levi out of the office.

"Do *not* let a call or anything else happen without contacting me immediately." Kennedy called after me. "You hear me?"

"Got it, Officer Kink. No worries." I hollered back and caught up with Levi as he stormed from the building. "Whoa, slow down. What's up your butt?" Laughing at my own choice of words, I sidled closer to Levi. "I mean, I know what *could* be up your butt. Or maybe what you might be thinking about putting up *my* butt." I knew I was playing with fire, but I'd never claimed to know when to shut up.

Levi whirled around and backed me into an alley. When my back met a brick wall, I noticed the fire in Levi's eyes. "Believe me, *kid*, I know exactly what I want and where I want it. Now is not the time for this conversation. I need you to take this stalker thing a bit more seriously." Levi's breathing was heavy as he fisted his hand in my hair and pulled my head to his shoulder. Holding me tight, Levi spoke against my head. "You can't joke your way out of this. Someone may be watching you or following you. You have to be vigilant and take it seriously. Okay?" His last word was a plea added to the end of his commands.

Swallowing hard, I nodded. "Yeah, okay. I can do that."

"Okay, then let's go eat dinner. You can tell Cody about everything so he can keep an eye out as well." Levi let me go and gestured toward B & B.

Minutes later, I'd settled beside Levi in a booth and our food arrived. Cody pulled a chair up to our table and Micah and Cole stopped by and joined the group as well. I quickly gave them a rundown of our visit with Kennedy.

"So, you don't think the handsy drunk guy from the bar has anything to do with the hang-ups?" Cody asked.

Shrugging, I stuffed three fries in my mouth. "Who knows," I said after swallowing. "But the guy at Strip Teaze has never caused any problems, doesn't send up warning signs like some others do, and has always been the type to follow the rules. Respectful. I really feel bad for him. He and his partner had been together for three years, I think."

"Other guys send up warning signs?" Levi demanded with wide eyes.

"Well, yeah." I answered before taking a big bite of my burger. Once I'd purposely taken an extra-long time to chew and swallow while Levi shot daggers my way the whole time, I continued my answer. "I mean, some guys are creeps, and you can tell from the moment they walk in. Others toe the line until they think they are owed something, then they get demanding and rough. The worst are the ones who look at you only as an object in a kinky fetish.

They think they can buy a private lap dance, slide an extra fifty into your shorts, and get lucky in the back room."

Levi's eyes were on fire and his skin flushed red from his chest up to his ears. He shot to his feet and walked out the backdoor of the B & B.

I grimaced at the guys. "I didn't mean to piss him off." Guilt ate at me. I'd simply been answering Levi's original question, I wasn't even trying to irritate him. I wiped my mouth and tossed the napkin to the table. "I'll go check on him."

Following the same trail Levi had taken, I pushed open the backdoor and found him pacing the alley behind Cody's restaurant. I eased into the alley and waited, hands in pockets. I stood against the brick building until Levi seemed to have calmed himself enough to speak.

He whirled on me with both arms crossed over his chest. Coming from anyone else, I likely would have felt intimidated, but I knew Levi would no sooner hurt me than cut off his drawing hand. His posture was his shield, his gruff attitude his protection, his harsh words his defense. "I don't like it."

I cocked my head to the side and waited for the words I predicted would come. *"I don't like you dancing, you can do so much better than selling your body."* I'd heard it so many times. Cutting Levi off with a raised hand, I saved him the energy of telling me how slutty and low-class dancing made me. "Before you go any further, let me just tell you. I love to dance. I know I could have another job, but I choose this one for now. It's my escape. Not a lot of people can say they love their work, but I do. I'm sorry if my choice of profession is beneath you, but I won't stop doing something I love for you."

Levi frowned and then rolled his eyes. "Would you shut up for a second?"

I lowered my gaze toward the ground. "I'm done."

"I know you love to dance, and I'd never ask you to stop or change unless it was something *you* wanted to do." Levi's stance relaxed slightly as his body moved toward mine by a microscopic inch. "You're one of the most talented and most gorgeous dancers I've ever had the privilege of knowing."

"You've never even been to Strip Teaze to watch me." My hands went to my hips.

"Doesn't matter that I've not watched you at work. I saw you at your birthday party. Plus, I've got two eyes and an appreciation for artistically beautiful things. I can see you. I watch your graceful movements. I know how free you are when you're dancing around the house to a favorite song."

Levi had slowly moved so close that I felt the heat of his body and smelled the light scent of his soap and deodorant on the air.

"What I don't like is that others think you owe them something or that they can take what they want from you. It kills me to think of men objectifying you, taking advantage of your kind spirit, or making you feel as if you're less than worthy of the best this world has to offer." Levi cupped my cheek and brushed a lock of hair from my forehead. "You deserve the best of everything in this life, and someday the perfect guy is going to give it all to you."

"I believe that." I smiled slightly. "I need to convince the guy he's the perfect one."

Levi shook his head. "I don't think it's me. I wish it were. I'd give you everything you deserve if I could." In a rare moment of vulnerability, Levi let down his guard. "You deserve it all and you deserve better than me."

"How about you let *me* decide what I deserve?" I reached for Levi's arm and trailed my hand down until our fingers met. "I don't know what got you thinking you're not pretty damn great, but I'm here to tell you that you *are*. Damn great, that is. You're a successful business owner and artist. You have the best fucking family and friends in the world supporting you. You live in a great little town that mostly accepts you for who you are. And you have a heart of gold and the fierceness of a lion when it comes to those you care about." I stepped closer, our bodies only a hair's width apart. I tipped my head up and found our lips within millimeters of contact. "And I'd be fuckin' blessed to have someone as amazing as you."

Levi sighed, his warm breath puffing on my skin. He rested his forehead against mine. "You make me sound pretty darn great." He chuckled. "But, I think maybe you're a bit biased."

"Nope." I reached up my arms, circling his neck to hug him close.

The moment had turned from borderline sexual a few moments before to intimately emotional as I reassured Levi of his worth. "I speak only the truth." I nuzzled my nose into his neck. "I may have a flair for theatrics, and I tend to add a little flair here and there, but the basis of what I said is one hundred percent true." Up on my tiptoes, I whispered in his ear, "You, Levi Wells, are downright fabulous and anyone would be lucky to call you theirs." Backing away, I paused for a brief moment and flashed a sly smile. "And, as fate would have it, my fabulousness is available for partnering up with your fabulousness. So, have your people call my people, dahling." I winked and grabbed his elbow. "Come on, they've probably eaten all our food by now."

We returned to our table.

Levi blushed, but I simply smiled smugly at the curious glances. The moment in the alley had been something private between Levi and me, and I planned to keep it that way.

CHAPTER 7

LEVI

My damp hands had taken on a tremor and my head pounded. Knowing Jay would be arriving soon was messing with me. Badly.

I'd done so many tattoos counting them all would be impossible. Tattoos on backs, ribs, butts, breasts, and nether regions. I'd done them all without a single thought or issue.

So how was a flashy, dramatic, annoying as hell twink getting a tattoo on my table bothering me so damn much? I'd had damn fine men on my table before and never even blinked. A few men, gay and straight, had found the experience of getting inked arousing and had a hard time hiding it. Again, didn't faze me.

But the thought of a shirtless Jay draped over my worktable, my hands caressing his skin to apply the design, my face close to his body and breathing in his scent, all of it was too much. My mind raced, and I thought of calling him to postpone the tattoo.

Ding-ding.

Too late.

Damn it.

That beautiful, frustrating, flamboyant queen sauntered into my shop. Thumbing the screen of his phone with a quick scowl, he pocketed the device before pinning his gaze on me.

"Hiya, Daddy." Jay brushed a light kiss across my cheek, ran a hand from my chest to my shoulder, and then continued his catwalk toward the appointment room. "Should I get naked now or wait until you can demand I strip?"

Fuck me. I wouldn't survive this tattoo.

I took a deep breath and followed Jay. "You can keep your pants on, just take off your shirt."

Jay turned around and crossed his arms. "What? I wore my cutest panties for you."

The little shit had the nerve to wink, lick his lips, and shimmy down the waistband of his track pants a couple inches so I could see teal and black zebra striped underwear.

"Pull up your damn pants." Breathing deeply, I steeled myself against the lust those underwear awakened. "I'm tattooing your back. You don't need to be naked. Just take off your shirt." I prepared my tools as a distraction, but a movement caught my eye. I turned in time to see Jay strip his tank over his head to reveal his perfect skin, flat stomach, and lean waist. The low-slung track pants showed the top of a light treasure trail and the beginning of the ever-tempting V of muscle.

"Like what you see?" Jay's words were followed by his hand tracing over his chest before he flicked a thumb over a nipple. "We could have some pre-tattoo fun right here." He reached behind his back to test the strength of the table. "I think it would hold up. What d'ya say, Daddy? Want to paint me with your gun?"

I shot from my stool and crowded into Jay's space until he was forced to step to the side. My breath came quickly and my hands acted on their own. I spun him to face me and pressed him a few more steps until his back bumped into the wall. As my hips pinned him against the wall, I groaned as Jay's hard cock rocked against mine. I ran my hands up his chest. With one hand moving to the back of his neck and the other reaching his head to take a fistful of hair, I gripped it and maneuvered him so my lips were right at his ear. I traced my tongue along the shell of Jay's ear until he whimpered.

"You're here for a tattoo, nothing more. Don't make me regret agreeing to ink you." I growled my words against his cheek and fought the temptation to take his mouth with mine. "And the day we finally do this it definitely won't be on a damn tattoo table. You deserve so damn much more than a quick fuck." Words flowed from my mouth, speaking from my heart and completely bypassing my brain. "You deserve a big comfortable bed, candles, and romance. When we do this, we will do it right. I promise to do right by you." The words shook me to the core, and I pushed away from Jay as if he were hot lava scalding my skin.

Holding my head in my hands, I spun around and attempted to get my breathing under control. "Fuck, we need to get started, but I need a minute."

Jay snorted behind me. "Damn sure I need more than a minute." He wisely gave me a wide berth as he walked from the room. "I'm going to go try to take a piss if I can get this fuckin' hard on out of the way."

While he was gone, I walked to my office, slurped the rest of my morning coffee, and chugged a bottle of water. Adjusting my dick, I walked from my office. "Get it together, Wells. You've got work to do."

Jay rounded the corner from the bathroom as I approached the appointment room. His gigantic, smug smile should have annoyed the hell out of me, but it did nothing more than warm my heart a lot more than I wanted it to.

"Since you're permanently inking my skin in a few moments, I'll let the last ten minutes go. For now." Jay walked closer, stopping inches from me. "But don't think I will *ever* forget the words you spoke. We *will* discuss further. But, later." Jay reached up and patted my cheek. "Right now, I feel like you need an emotional break. And I need my tattoo. Let's go, Daddy."

Jay turned on his heel and sauntered into the room to sprawl himself across the table. "Where do you want me?"

I ignored the sexual connotation in his words. "Actually, I'm switching you to the chair so I can get your back at a better angle." As soon as I had Jay seated with his back to me, and I started prepping his skin for the design, I fell into my normal routine. The sights, sounds, and scents filling the room calmed me. The touch of my skin rubbing over the transfer paper as I placed the design on Jay's back had an immediate grounding effect. Peeling the paper away to reveal what was possibly my best artwork to date sent a shiver of anxious anticipation through my body.

I wanted Jay. It seemed as if my inner psyche had plans for the near future with Jay. But, my professional and artistic side pushed those thoughts from my head—at least for the time I had Jay under my gun. Picking up the cool, heavy piece of machinery, I let the lulling buzz ease my remaining twitch of nerves. "Okay, so I'm starting with the basic design outline today. In another session, I'll do the shading and shadows and precise details." I finished readying my supply table. "I don't expect you to have any problems with the gun, but if the pain gets to be too much, you can stop and take a few breathers. I tell people the sensation is similar to a fine-point ink pen writing heavily on a sunburn."

"Sounds lovely." Jay chuckled. "Let's get started."

With that, I entered the relaxed and focused cloud that always took over when I tattooed a client. I was completely tuned into Jay's verbal and nonverbal cues, but I found myself living in a separate world as my gun deposited ink into his skin as smoothly as he'd deposited himself into my life.

I stopped several times during the two-hour tattoo to check on Jay and make sure he was okay. Each time, I got a murmur of agreement. By the time I was rinsing his back and slathering on the ointment, I almost thought he had fallen asleep.

"Oh my god, that feels so good. Like a good hurt. It's cool, like it's soothing. Can you keep doing it the rest of the day?"

Jay's groggy voice startled me, causing me to stop mid-rub along his back's red and irritated skin.

"Damn, man, I almost thought you'd decided to take a nap." I finished applying the ointment and began to prepare the plastic wrap that Jay would need on the tattoo for at least the rest of the day. "Shit, I almost forgot to ask. Do you want to see it now or wait until it's done?"

Jay shifted on the reclined chair, groaning as if awakening from a leisurely rest. "That was the weirdest experience I've ever had. I felt each and every scrape and scratch of the needle, and the parts that went over bone were a bitch, but I'm not sure I've ever felt more relaxed. Like the pain eventually turned to almost a hypnotic pleasure. And the buzz of the gun was like a lullaby I couldn't escape." He stood slowly, holding the chair for balance.

"Yeah, it's the endorphins. A lot of people can fall into a relaxed state during a tattoo." I reached for his elbow to steady him. "Careful. You've been sitting a long time. Get your bearings before you try to go too far."

"I think I want to see it. What's easiest? Give me a mirror or take a picture?" Jay moved from the chair and attempted to look into the wall mirror.

"Probably easiest to have me take a picture." I grabbed my phone. "Hold still. I'll take a couple."

After snapping a few shots, I handed the phone to Jay. "Now, don't forget, this is the outline. It will look a ton better and very different once we ink the shading and finer details."

"It's beautiful. I already know it and I haven't even seen it yet." Jay reached for my phone. "Oh my god, Levi, it's amazing. I knew it would be."

His words trembled and a hand flew to cover his mouth.

"I think it's one of my best pieces to date. I'm definitely damn proud of it." What would Jay think of the final piece? *Fragile strength* still needed to be added along with finishing touches. I took back the phone and texted the pictures to Jay's number. "Now, let me get you all wrapped up. You can't be on your back for a couple days." The moment I said the words I knew Jay would have a comeback.

"Mmmm, no activities that require me on my back. Guess I'll have to play cowboy or doggy for a while." Jay tossed a sultry glance over his shoulder and wiggled his nose.

"I was thinking more along the lines of when you're sleeping." I chose to ignore his comment. "You can sleep on your side, but stay off your back for a while." I covered the fresh ink with plastic wrap and taped the edges. "You'll need to wash it with antibacterial soap and warm water starting tomorrow. And you'll need to keep it covered in the ointment. I usually suggest the soap and ointment for about three or four days, but if it's still got some spots healing or scabbing up, you can do it longer, up to a week." I handed Jay the tube of ointment I'd used and grabbed a bottle of antibacterial soap. I didn't usually give these items to clients, but I knew Jay's money situation was tight.

"So, do I need to get a back scrubber or something?" Jay moved slowly as he gingerly attempted to pull his tank over his head.

"No, don't scrub it. Let the skin heal on its own. It will heal similar to a sunburn. There will be peeling and itching. Keeping it moist will help with the itching." I cleaned up the supplies. The work *after* a tattoo was almost as detailed as the actual tattoo.

"But," Jay furrowed his brow, "how am I supposed to wash my back?"

I rolled my eyes as I threw away discarded paper towels and glanced at him, expecting to see a teasing grin, but his expression was serious. "How do you normally wash your back?"

"I mean, I guess I pour soap on a loofah and hope for the best." Jay shrugged. "I don't do a ton of back detail work. But, now I need to make sure I'm getting it clean so it doesn't get infected, right?"

"Well, yeah, but an infection is pretty rare unless you're rolling in the dirt or wiping germs directly on it." I smiled at the adorable look of worry that decorated Jay's face. "How about I come over and make sure it's clean tomorrow morning?" Where the hell that offer came from I'd never know.

"Would you really do that?" Jay's voice was thick with emotion.

"Sure. My shop only stays in business if clients are happy and if the tattoos look amazing, so making sure your tat heals well benefits us both." I raised a shoulder. I was sure my interest in going to Jay's place in the morning had *nothing* to do with anything but his after-care.

"Can I watch you clean up?" Jay hopped up on the table.

"Are you okay? Feeling dizzy?" I stood from my stool and stepped toward him. Touching his forehead, I sought his pulse with my other hand.

"Yeah, I'm good. I'm feeling totally euphoric and sluggish right now. And I'm interested in watching you work." Jay closed his eyes and smiled sleepily as he nuzzled a cheek into my palm. "I almost feel like I've danced for four hours and the adrenaline rush is still keeping me high, but I know the crash is coming soon."

"Well, in that case, you can watch me clean up." I glanced at my watch. "Did you walk? I don't have another appointment today. Want to grab something to eat? Some water and food may help avoid the crash."

Jay nodded, his eyes sleepy. "Sounds good."

By the time I'd finished sanitizing, refilling, and prepping supplies, I saw Jay curled into a ball on the table sound asleep. Jostling him gently, I took his hand and let him lean on me as I led him to my office. "Drink this water and then sleep a little more." I handed the kid a bottle of water and watched him chug it down before he snuggled onto the cushions on his left side.

An hour later, I was all caught up on paperwork and had completely straightened my office as Jay began to stir. "You still want to grab some food? Or would you rather go home and veg out?"

Jay sat up, wincing at what I knew was a very tender back, and yawned. "Food sounds good."

The kid was a bottomless pit.

I locked up the shop and led Jay to the parking lot. We headed toward the B & B, but at the last minute I turned the truck toward the highway.

"Where are we going?" Jay was attempting to find a comfortable position to sit without hurting his back.

"Decided we needed a change of scenery. You like Chinese?" My heart smiled at the impromptu dinner date, but my brain was cursing me.

"Love it." Jay smiled.

Thirty minutes down the road, I pulled into a little run-down looking place that I knew had the best Chinese food around. The drive had been comfortable, full of random chatter and laughter. Jay was an easy person to be around once I realized I didn't have to keep my guard up quite so high.

"Hey." Jay's words were a strangled whisper as his hand reached for mine.

The atmosphere in the truck immediately shifted. Jay's eyes met mine and, in that moment, I knew I'd do absolutely anything he asked of me. Something had changed between us. Slowly. Persistently. Like the slow pressing blade of a glacier against dirt and rock. And, just like glaciers only move one way, I knew things between Jay and I were moving forward whether I was on board or not. But, the thing was, while my head still wanted to fight it, my heart had admitted defeat. Squeezing his hand, I rasped out, "What?"

Jay scooted across the seat until he was mere inches from me. "Today has been pretty epic. I mean, it's been a fairly normal day in so many ways, but I feel like it's been a pivotal point in my life, as well."

Having no idea where he was going with his words, I waited patiently.

"I know you think it's maybe not the best idea. And, I've told you I'll wait. But, um, I was wondering if you'd…um, maybe…I mean, only if you want to…um, would you want to…"

Jay's words tumbled out as sweet, innocent, and unsure as I'd ever heard him. Without giving it a second thought, I cupped Jay's face in my hand and brushed my lips across his. His gasp of breath, the little whimper from his throat, and the sweet taste of his mouth brought me back for a deeper, more thorough kiss. Never had there been a more perfect kiss. My tongue traced his lips, tangled with his tongue, and soothed the sting from my nibbling teeth. All time stood still. Careful of his back, I wrapped him in my arms and pulled him over onto my lap.

Jay's arms held tight around my neck. His lips pulled from mine as he backed away a sliver and stared deeply into my eyes. With a strangled chuckle that sounded very close to a choked sob, Jay's mouth dropped back to mine, and we lost ourselves in the kiss once again.

A white-hot flash of light outside lit up the truck, followed almost immediately by a ground-shaking clash of thunder.

No, our kiss wasn't moving the heavens and earth, it was a pop-up thunderstorm.

I laughed against Jay's mouth. "If we want any chance of getting our food without being soaking wet, we better move now." The kiss had ended, but would never be forgotten, as I tumbled from the truck and made a run for it as the skies opened up and the deluge descended.

CHAPTER 8

JAY

Best. Fucking. Day. *Ever.*

Finally got a tattoo.

Had the most amazing natural high I'd ever experienced.

Kissed and kissed by a guy I'd lusted after for over two years. A guy I was one hundred percent head-over-heels...in love with? At least in *major* like.

And now what would be the best Chinese food ever.

At least the Chinese food would always stick in my mind as the best ever because I was floating on cloud nine with no intent of coming down anytime soon.

Did I mention I made out with fucking Levi Wells?

I traced a finger over my still-tingling lips and smiled.

"Earth to Jay." Levi nudged me.

I caught his blush and smirk and couldn't help but smile and feel the heat rush to my own cheeks.

"What do you want to eat?"

I glanced at the menu. The restaurant was set up like a fast food place as far as putting in your order, but the meal was brought to your table if you decided to dine-in. "Ugh, I don't know. Everything looks so damn good."

"Anything you *don't* like?" Levi cocked a brow.

"No," I bit my lip to hide a suggestive smile. "I'm easy."

Levi shook his head and turned to place our order. "Sesame chicken, orange chicken, Asian chicken, vegetable lo mein, white rice, crab rangoon, and two egg rolls."

My stomach growled at the thought of our delicious dinner. Panicking for a moment when I saw the total, I reached for my wallet silently praying I'd have enough to cover my part.

"I got this." Levi elbowed me away and handed his card to the employee.

Blushing even harder because I was pretty damn sure moths would have flown from my wallet when I cracked it open, I mumbled, "Thanks."

"Go find a seat. I'll grab silverware and napkins." Levi nodded toward the dining area.

I gladly took the suggestion for what it was: an escape, a diversion, and Levi's way of easing my discomfort over him paying for our meal.

Why did Levi paying bother me so much? All the guys had given me food gift certificates for my birthday. Cody often comped my food at the B & B or sent me home with so many leftovers I ate for days to come. And Micah had bought my food more times than I could count.

But, eating with Levi alone was different. We weren't at our usual B & B. It wasn't the whole gang. And, what else was different? Oh yeah, we'd had our tongues down each other's throats. This moment seemed a whole lot like a date. And that had me feeling…I wasn't exactly sure how I was feeling. Embarrassed I didn't have money to feed myself? Touched that Levi automatically wanted to pay? Embarrassed again because Levi more than likely automatically knew I was broke? Silly and ridiculous for making such a big deal out of the guy buying a simple dinner? Yes. The answer was yes to all of the above.

I grabbed a seat in the back corner of the almost deserted restaurant.

As our order arrived, we made room for the massive amount of food filling the table.

I watched Levi knock over the soy sauce and barely catch the napkins before they fell to the floor and realized he was likely feeling as off-kilter after our time together as I was. "Are we going to talk about today?"

"No." Keeping his gaze on his plate, Levi shoveled Asian chicken and rice into his mouth.

"No?" My word squeaked and my stomach plummeted. Was Levi going to act as if the whole wonderful, glorious day hadn't happened?

"Nope." Levi smirked at me. "Right now, we're eating. Then we're going back to your place. We'll talk there then I'll go home. Tomorrow morning I'll come check on your tattoo." He shoved an eggroll my way. "But, right now, we eat."

My studio apartment was tiny, but I kept it neat and homey. It was a comfortable place to call home and I was proud of the few great pieces of furniture I'd snagged at thrift stores. My interior decorating style was a mishmash of contemporary and eclectic with touches of shabby chic. I basically used whatever I could find; if I liked it, I used it.

Unlocking the door to my place and having Levi follow me inside was yet another surreal experience in my already hard-to-believe day. When

Levi walked past me and stood in the middle of the room glancing around curiously, I couldn't help but stare at him.

"What?" He smiled.

"I can't believe you're in my apartment."

"It's nice. Cute. Suits you." Levi continued looking around.

Snapping out of my trance, I stepped forward. "Let me give you the grand tour," I joked, gesturing around the room with my hand. "This is my bedroom, living room, kitchen, and bathroom."

Levi laughed. "It's great. You have room for your dance materials and supplies along with your makeup." His gaze had wandered to my closet where loads of shimmery costumes were spilling out next to my tiny dresser.

It held the remnants of seven drag queens putting on their faces.

"You've made good use of your space."

I felt my cheeks heat, and I cleared my throat. "Um, thanks. You want something to drink?"

"No, I want to take a quick look at your tattoo, and then I better head out."

I knew my face spoke volumes of my disappointment.

Levi noticed immediately and placed a comforting hand on my shoulder.

He ushered me to the bathroom and turned me to face the mirror before lifting my shirt to inspect his handiwork of tape and plastic. "Listen, I don't think me staying tonight is wise. I'll come back in the morning to help you take care of the ink. For tonight, if you can stand to keep on the bandage it will help reduce the chance of your shirt or sheet sticking to you. Make sure you wear something old, since there's a good likelihood the skin will ooze a bit and the ink will run off on your shirt." Levi finished checking my back and returned my shirt to its original position.

"Really thought the first time you lifted up my shirt would end much differently," I mumbled, pouting into the mirror as I watched Levi.

He reached for my shoulders and turned me around. "First times aren't only times. We've got time. I don't feel like rushing into things would be good."

"Yeah, you're right, two plus years is a little too fast." My sarcasm wasn't lost on Levi.

"*You* may have been thinking about whatever this is," Levi gestured between us, "for more than two years. But, you've got to give me some time. I'm an old man, and I need time to adjust to changes." Levi winked.

I curled my lip and wrinkled my nose. "I think this is the first time I've not been totally into you being older. Plenty of guys would jump feet first, eyes closed, and never even consider the pros or cons."

Levi brushed a thumb along my cheekbone. "Those guys are idiots who wouldn't give a shit about you or doing things right." He took both of my hands in his before drawing in a deep breath and letting it out slowly. "If we're doing this, we're doing it right. I don't jump into things. I think things through. So, you can be assured, if we come to a mutual decision that we're going to stop fighting it and give this thing a go, that I'm one hundred percent on board and willing to make it work."

My heart fluttered for a few seconds before my brain registered what he was saying. "So, there's still a chance you'll say I'm not your type and you're too old and we can't take a chance and see where things go?" The quiver of my lip proceeded the sting of tears in the back of my throat.

"*Chance* isn't even the right word. *Fact* is more accurate." Levi's attempt at a straight face morphed into a smirk. "I'll say until I'm blue in the face that you're not my type, and I'm too old for you." He caressed my cheek.

"What about taking that risk?" My words were barely a whisper.

"If I were a betting man, I'd place my money on taking that risk." Levi leaned in to brush a soft kiss across my lips. "And maybe the fact that you're not my type, and I'm way too old for you makes the bet so much more appealing."

Wrapping my arms around Levi's neck and jumping up to pretzel my legs around his waist, I threw my head back in laughter as Levi kissed my neck and spun me to place my ass on the bathroom counter.

Staying clear of my tender back, Levi grasped my hips and pulled close. "This right here is exactly why I can't stay. We'd end up doing something we'd both enjoy, but then at least one of us would regret it terribly because it's not the way I want things to happen."

With my bottom lip caught between my teeth, I smiled seductively. "So, you're saying you've thought about what you'd like to happen? You've thought about us?"

"Only on every day that ends in Y." Levi growled against my ear before his sweet, warm lips captured mine in a slow, sweet kiss. Easing back from the kiss Levi spoke softly. I've accepted I can't fight this. But, I need you to accept that it needs to move at my pace. I'm not saying like molasses, but not like a racecar." With one more kiss, Levi released me. "Can you do that for me?"

Nodding dumbly, I squeaked, "Yes, Daddy." He hadn't completely kissed the sass out of me.

Levi rolled his eyes and chuckled. "That damn mouth will get you in trouble."

Licking my lips before smooching the air, I winked. "I'd be happy to show you how much trouble this mouth of mine can get into."

Levi headed toward the door before calling over his shoulder. "I'm leaving now."

"See you in the morning?" I still couldn't believe I was saying those words to the object of my affection after all the time I'd patiently waited. *Finally*.

My phone rang and Levi paused in the doorway. Glancing at the screen after I pulled it from my pocket, I immediately schooled my face. I ignored the call and started to speak to Levi, but the damn call came in again.

Levi scowled and held out his hand for the phone. "Is it him?"

I shrugged. "Probably," I lied. I knew it was him. I handed the phone to Levi and scolded myself for feeling guilty.

"Hello?" Levi growled into the phone and then he was silent, listening. "Listen you piece of shit, if you know what's good for you, you'll lose this number and forget he ever existed." Levi listened intently for a few more seconds before he hung up. "Damn it!" He handed the phone back to me. "How many times has he called since you told Kennedy about it?"

I lifted a defiant shoulder in response.

"How. Many. Times?" Levi's words left no doubt he was pissed and concerned.

"Just twice. Once earlier today and then just now." Why did it seem like *I* was the one in the wrong?

"Was that who was on the phone when you came in the shop today?"

Levi's words dripped in disbelief and disappointment. I felt like a total heel, and I could only nod my head in answer.

"And you didn't feel the need to let me know?"

"I guess not. I mean, I was too pumped up for the tattoo and getting to spend the day with you. I didn't want to ruin it by whining about some harmless phone calls." My excuse sounded whiny and flimsy even to my own ears.

"Kennedy *told* you to let him know if the calls came again."

"I know, okay? I didn't want to postpone the tattoo to go tell Kennedy. I'll tell him tonight." I took a deep breath, angry that the evening had taken a negative turn. All because of some stupid phone calls that probably didn't mean a single thing.

"Damn straight you'll tell him. I'm not leaving until you make the call." Levi crossed his arms over his chest and jutted out his chin.

Damn stubborn-ass man.

"Fine, fine," I muttered while I pulled my phone out again and made the call. Waiting for Kennedy to answer, I watched Levi while my feelings battled inside. On one hand, I was annoyed at his bossy, demanding attitude and I was *beyond* frustrated with the stupid phone calls. On the other hand, I couldn't help but appreciate that Levi was concerned and wanted to be sure I was safe and protected. I'd never had that growing up and it warmed my heart to receive it from Levi.

"Marks," Kennedy's gruff voice answered.

"Kennedy, it's Jay," I stated softly.

"What's up, kiddo?" At that moment, as I stood under Levi's watchful glare and listened to Kennedy's attentive voice, I hated that reminder of how much younger I was, of how much they still saw me as a child. If I were older, more mature, more experienced at life, would the phone calls still be happening? If so, would I be more able to "man up" and take care of them myself? Was I some pathetic little homo who couldn't even defend himself against some heavy breathing and hang-ups?

Levi cleared his throat and pulled me from my self-loathing.

"Oh, um, I needed let you know that I got two more calls today. One was earlier and one was a couple minutes ago. Both were different numbers. I'll text the numbers to you when we hang up. The first call was the usual breathing and hang up. The second call I actually declined. Then he called again. Levi answered. Levi threatened him and he hung up like all the other times." I heard the click of Kennedy's keyboard as he recorded what I was saying.

"Did you hear any background noise?"

"I didn't." I repeated the question to Levi, he shook his head. "Levi didn't either."

"Okay. For now, we keep a record of the calls and anything that changes. Unless we can trace the numbers, there's not a lot we can do."

Kennedy's words reflected his frustration with the situation.

"It's okay, I wasn't hurt. They're some stupid calls." I tried to assure Kennedy as much as I said the words for myself and for Levi.

Levi stepped forward and grabbed the phone. "There's seriously nothing that can be done?" He listened to Kennedy's answer, which was likely the same thing he'd said to me. Pinching the bridge of his nose, Levi let out a deep breath. "Yeah, okay. Thanks." He ended the call and handed back the phone. "Maybe I should stay?" Levi's brows scrunched together.

"Nope. No way." I shook my head and ushered him toward the door. "You wouldn't stay earlier, you don't get to stay now just because you think I'm some little pathetic gay boy who can't take care of himself."

"Damn it. Stop pushing me." Levi grunted and whirled around to face me. "I don't think that about you." He cupped my cheek. "Never have, never will." Brushing hair from my forehead with his other hand, Levi cocked his head to the side. "I worry. I want you safe."

I softened at his words. "Thank you, that means a lot." I nuzzled my cheek against his hand. "But, you were right about what you said earlier. I know you don't want to rush things and you need some time. I don't want you staying with me out of some feeling of obligation. When you stay over or I stay at yours, I want it to be mutually agreed upon and for the right reasons." I kissed his palm. "I'm heading to bed as soon as you leave. I'll be fine. You'll be here in the morning to check on my tattoo."

"I'll be here to check on *you*," Levi insisted.

I couldn't help but smile at how quickly he was moving even though he swore we were taking it slow. A couple hours before he'd offered to come check my ink. Now he was promising it was *me* he was coming to check on.

"Will you at least let me look at all the windows and be sure they are locked?"

"Yes, that's fine. I mean, you can inspect all three windows, two of which are painted completely shut. But, if it makes you feel better, be my guest." I gestured to the window in the kitchen, the one that sort of divided my bedroom from my living room, and the tiny one in the corner bathroom. No one older than a toddler would be able to fit through that one.

Levi walked to all three windows and assured himself they were locked and secure. "I want the chain, the door lock, and the deadbolt put on before I walk away from your door." He headed toward the exit, but turned to kiss my cheek and pull me into a hug before he opened the door. "Can you *promise* you'll call me or Kennedy, or even one of the others, if something happens or even just feels weird?"

"Yes, I promise." I snuggled against his warm, comforting strength. "Now, get going so I can lock the door." Once I'd closed the door behind him, I made a big production of announcing each lock as I slid them into place. "Locked up tight as a chastity belt," I sassed through the door and heard Levi chuckle.

I stood by the door until I heard his truck pull away then I turned to prepare for bed. Fifteen minutes later, as I climbed under the sheets, my phone buzzed with a text from Levi.

I'm home. Sleep tight. See you in the morning.

The words were sweet and comforting. But the little heart he'd included in the message would be floating through my dreams all night. I replied.

Can't wait.

Maybe the kissy face I sent with my words was over the top, but I wasn't above letting emoticons represent my deep-down feelings. Smiling to myself, I snuggled into the blankets and let the excitement of the day give way to total exhaustion.

Best. Day. Ever.

CHAPTER 9

LEVI

Sleep was a long time coming once I got home from Jay's place. The rest I *did* get was interrupted with fits of wakefulness in which I checked my phone and debated on contacting Jay to see if he was okay. Morning came and I bounded from bed with purposeful intent. I had a couple things I wanted to do before I headed to Jay's.

Grabbing a quick shower, I skipped coffee and thumbed through my phone as I ambled toward my truck. I had Chuck's name in my phone because I'd done the most recent of his many tattoos. Pressing the CALL button, I waited for Jay's boss at Strip Teaze to answer.

"Chuck here."

"Chuck, Levi Wells. How's it going?" I wouldn't call the man a friend per say, but a good guy and he ran his business with integrity from what I'd gathered over the years.

"Wells? Hell, to what do I owe the honor?" Chuck's usual good-natured smile could be heard in his words.

"I was wondering if you'd thought about keeping Jay Owens off work maybe a week longer. With pay of course. The kid needs the money." I cut straight to the chase.

There was a long pause on the other end of the line. "Can't say I'd thought any about it, no. Why?"

"He got more phone calls yesterday." I climbed in my truck and turned the phone to speaker. "Thought maybe another week out of the public eye would help take the spotlight off him."

"Gotta tell ya, Wells, I'm losing money having him out as it is. He's got regulars, and he brings in a lot of business." Chuck's words held the weight of an internal battle. "I mean, I don't want to bring him back in if it's going to put him in danger. I take care of my staff, you know that."

"I do. That's why I wanted to put the idea to you." I backed out of the garage and pointed my truck toward BJ's little coffee and pastry shop. "Jay would never ask for more time off. He needs the money too badly and doesn't want to admit that the calls are bothering him."

"Well, shit. Yeah, another week won't hurt. I'll let him know he needs to take the extra days." Chuck sighed. "But, damn, I hate to lose money."

"Just think of how much money you'd lose if you didn't have Jay permanently," I grimly reminded Chuck.

"Good point, good point." Chuck agreed.

I ended the call as I pulled up to the coffee shop. The Steaming Mug wasn't the only place in BJ to get coffee, but it was the trendiest and most popular with the younger crowd. I ordered a sweet coffee, a sweet hot tea, two pastries, and two breakfast sandwiches figuring I'd drink whichever one Jay didn't want. Balancing the drink carrier and bag, I climbed back into the truck, secured our breakfast, and headed toward Jay's place.

The drive was short, but gave me plenty of time to overthink. I wracked my brain trying to pinpoint the moment when Jay had gone from just an annoyance to something more. But, no specific time came to mind. He had slowly eaten away at my defenses until I could no longer fight his charismatic personality. Was I taking a stupid risk or making a sound decision? Were my feelings toward him based on physical wants and desires, or was I drawn to him as a person no matter his appearance and his age?

I ran a hand over my face as I slowed at a stop sign. Was I having a mid-life crisis? Was I finding myself attracted to Jay because he was young and energetic and made me feel my own youth? Fuck, I was barely into my thirties, it wasn't as if I was pushing senior citizen status. Yes, Jay was young, but that didn't make me *old,* did it?

A knock on my window scared the shit out of me and I jumped a foot off the seat before turning to see Micah standing by my truck. Checking my mirrors first, I rolled down the window. "Damn it, man. You scared the piss outta me."

"I had to. You'd been sitting here for about five minutes. I was afraid you'd get rear-ended or something. Where'd your mind go?" My cousin cocked his head.

Glancing in my mirror to be sure no one was behind me, I took a deep breath and gestured toward the passenger side. "Get in."

Micah smiled and shook his head, but sauntered to the other door and climbed in. "Aw, did you buy me breakfast? That's so sweet."

I flipped him the bird and drove toward Cody's B & B. "I'm guessing you were heading for coffee, right?"

"Yeah. But, I can drink whatever you got me." Micah winked.

"It's not for you and you know it," I growled out. Pulling the truck into the B & B parking lot, I knew the drinks and sandwiches would be cold if I talked to Micah for too long. "I'm heading over to Jay's to check on his fresh tattoo."

"Since when does a home check and delivered breakfast come with your work?"

I rolled my eyes. "It doesn't. At least not until this time."

"So, what? You got Jay naked on your table and couldn't resist?" Micah chuckled at the scowl I gave him.

"Damn it, don't even say that. And why would he be *naked* on my table? It was a back tattoo, nothing more." Locking my hands behind my head, I looked to the ceiling and breathed deeply.

"Did something go wrong? Is that why you're checking on him?" Micah seemed truly concerned.

"No, the tattoo went fine. He was asking how he was supposed to wash his back and not use a scrubber and the words tumbled from my mouth that I'd come over and check on the ink." I scrubbed my hands over my face.

"And it's just the ink you're checking on?" Micah's quiet question went straight to the heart of the matter.

"No. Not just the ink." I gestured toward the B & B. "You better go in and get your coffee."

Micah watched me for the span of several seconds. "It's okay to like him."

I turned to meet his gaze. "Yeah? Doesn't make me an old pervert going after a younger guy?"

Micah laughed. "No, definitely not an old pervert. Even if you were twenty years older. You're not after him for just sex. Although I'm sure that will end up being sweet, kinky, and fabulous, but you've been falling for him for a long time. It's okay to see where things might go."

My cousin's words soothed the part of my brain that was questioning my every move regarding Jay. "Thanks, man. That's good to hear."

Micah climbed from the truck. "Thanks for the ride. Tell Jay good morning for me."

I smiled at the thought of our little group of six all partnering up. Was it a given that we'd all gravitate toward each other? Micah was my cousin, Cody my best friend, it was natural that we all stayed close as we grew up. But, having Cole, Kennedy, and Jay enter our little circle almost seemed like fate. The BJ Boys expanding and settling down? Who would have ever thought it?

I pulled up to Jay's apartment and couldn't help but grin at the slight movement behind the curtain of his front window. Knowing he'd been waiting on me made my chest swell and my heart pound a little harder.

I gathered our little feast and took the stairs two at a time. Before I could even knock, Jay swung the door open.

"Good morning." He bit his lip and blushed through his words.

Had I not had my hands full of beverages and breakfast, I would have grabbed the little imp up in a full-on hug. "Hey, breakfast is served." I held up the bag and drink tray. "Hope you haven't already eaten."

Jay beamed. "Nah, I skip breakfast a lot of the times. Sometimes I get home so late from work that I sleep way past a decent breakfast time so I go for lunch." He reached for the bag and peered inside as he walked toward his little kitchen corner. "Mmmm, smells delish."

"Which drink do you want? I grabbed a tea and a coffee figuring I'd drink whichever one you didn't want." I held up the two for him to see.

"Chai tea latte?" Jay's expression was hopeful.

I nodded and had to chuckle as he clapped his hands before taking the proffered beverage with glee. "I freakin' love chai tea lattes." He took a sip before looking at me. "Wait, do you like the coffee one?"

Smiling, I nodded my head. "Yep, I got two that I would like no matter which one you chose." I grabbed the bag and unloaded the food. "Let's eat."

Jay caught me from behind, his long, lean arms wrapping around my middle and his cheek resting against my back. "Thank you for breakfast. No one has ever brought me breakfast before."

I turned in his arms and held his waist firmly as I backed him toward the tiny kitchen counter. "You deserve to have breakfast delivered every morning." Lifting him gently, careful of his back, I settled him on the counter and nestled my hips between his legs. When Jay's arms came up to snake around my neck, I dropped my lips to brush against his mouth. "Good morning." My gruff whisper sent shivers through Jay as he accepted my tongue into his mouth. He tasted of sweet mint and forbidden pleasure. And, damn, I wanted more. So much more.

When the kiss ended, we were both breathing hard and it took every ounce of my strength not to dry hump the kid right on his kitchen counter.

"I don't need the daily breakfast sandwiches, but the caffeinated beverage and a kiss like that will do nicely." Jay winked as he rubbed two fingers against his lips.

"Micah says hi." I moved to the tiny table and dug into the food.

"Yeah?" Jay smiled. "Micah's a good guy. Your entire little group are good guys."

"You know, I was sort of thinking about that this morning." I sipped my coffee. "You're pretty much part of that little group, you know that, right?"

"Can I call myself a BJ Boy?" Jay asked hopefully.

I laughed at his eagerness. "We'll see." I winked. "How's your back?"

"It's worse today than yesterday." Jay winced. "Feels like a bad sunburn. It's hot and itchy, and this morning my shirt was *stuck* to the oozy juices. Disgusting! I had to wet it to get the cloth unstuck. And you were right; the ink totally stained my shirt."

I smirked as Jay described his new ink. "Well, it *is* an open wound. Very superficial, but still an open wound. That's why it needs to be taken care of so it doesn't get infected. Finish up and I'll take a look."

"I'm going to save my pastry until later." Jay popped the last bite of sandwich in his mouth and stood from the table. He pulled his shirt over his head, revealing once again a taut, smooth stomach, indented with subtle ropes of muscle, a sprinkling of fine hair, and those damn V lines.

Swallowing down my food and the lustful longing that shot through my veins, I moved to study Jay's back. His skin was slightly irritated, but the ink looked good. "This looks fine, completely normal. I can help you wash it and smear the ointment."

Jay turned and gave me a wicked smile. "Does that mean we're showering together?" he purred.

"No." I chuckled. "I can wash your back without being in the shower."

"Darn." Jay pouted, but smiled a second later and grabbed his tea to finish it off.

His phone vibrated on the table and I stopped in my clearing of our trash to watch him answer. My gut tightened in anticipation of it being one of the hang-ups again. But Jay's eyes flashed recognition of the number and he answered it with a cheerful. "Hey, babe, you miss me already?" Jay's face brightened at first, but then his eyes zeroed in on me and his smile turned to a scowl. "Really? Well, that's very kind of you. Yes, I'm sure I'll have plenty to say to him. Yeah, see you then." Jay ended the call and pursed his lips as he studied me.

"What? Who was that? Why do you look pissed?" I knew it wasn't the anonymous caller, but I wasn't sure who Jay had been speaking to and why he looked as if he wanted to harm me.

"Did you speak to my boss?" Jay's words were slow and measured.

Ah, Chuck. Whew, for a moment I had been worried. "Chuck? Yeah, I talked to him this morning."

"Well, that was him. He informed me I could have another week off with pay since the calls haven't stopped." Jay put both hands on his hips. "Told me I should tell you thank you."

I smirked. "Don't have to thank me. Just enjoy your time and let's hope keeping you out of the public eye for another week will cool the caller down."

Jay threw his hands up in the air. "Of course I'm not going to *thank* you!" He jabbed my chest with a finger. "How could you do this?"

"Do what? Get you another week off with pay? Yeah, that was a really shitty thing to do." I rolled my eyes, not really sure why Jay was upset.

"You called my boss behind my back!"

"It wasn't like it was a secret. You just didn't happen to be there when I called." I shrugged.

"So, what? Now I'm like the little woman who can't make her own decisions? Or maybe you see me as a child who needs his parents to pave the way or get him out of jams?" Jay fumed. "I'm a freakin' adult, Levi. I don't need you calling my place of employment and getting me special treatment!"

Taken aback by his words, I paused momentarily before my own anger began to boil.

"Oh, well, fuckin' excuse me for caring! Pardon me for wanting to make sure you're safe. My bad for being worried about you and wanting to protect you." Scowling, I pointed a finger at Jay. "For someone who wanted to play the whole *Daddy* game, you sure don't seem to be very on board with me taking on that role."

Jay winced slightly and took a deep, calming breath.

I stepped toward him. "Look, I didn't mean to overstep. Let me wash your back..."

Jay put up a hand to stop me. "No, I need to be alone. I can handle my own back. Thanks for breakfast."

"Are you kicking me out?" I wasn't sure what to think.

"I need some time to think." Jay frowned. "We can talk later, okay?"

"You still want to work on your tattoo next week?" I was confused at being dismissed and an unfamiliar pain shot through my heart. I thought I'd been helping, but I'd pissed Jay off which had *not* been my intention at all.

"Yeah, for sure." Jay nodded and followed me to the door.

Leaning in to kiss Jay, I frowned when he offered his cheek rather than accepting my lips. "I'll talk to you later," I whispered.

Jay nodded and I turned to leave. Once I heard the sound of each lock engage, I headed toward my truck. What the actual fuck had just happened?

I found my truck pulling into the B & B with no actual idea of how I'd gotten there. Wandering into the restaurant, I glanced around for Cody. I must have looked bad because Cody took one look and gestured for me to head to his office. Five minutes later, he joined me with two piping hot cups of coffee.

"Damn man, you look like shit. What happened?" Cody handed me a cup and I sagged onto his office couch.

"I'm not even sure." I sipped the coffee and welcomed the stinging burn against my lips, tongue, and throat.

"Start at the beginning. I got all the time in the world to listen." Cody sat across from me and waited patiently.

"So, I guess Jay and I are maybe going to try this thing. Slowly." I began and glanced at Cody to see how he'd react. He nodded as if he'd expected me to say that the whole time. "He's still getting the calls. Chuck at Strip Teaze gave him a week off with pay, but since the calls are still happening, I called Chuck this morning and convinced him to give Jay another week with pay."

Cody cringed.

"What?"

"Nothing, go on." Cody prompted.

"I took him breakfast this morning so I could check on his tattoo. Things were going great. He was all for me joining him in the shower even though I assured him I could wash his back without getting in completely." I thought about the events that led up to Jay telling me to leave. "Chuck called, told him he could have another week. That's when Jay blew up. He was mad I called Chuck."

"Can you blame him?" Cody's words were not what I wanted to hear. I wanted him to be on my side. I was the one who was doing the right thing here. Jay was throwing a tantrum like a child.

"What? Is it wrong that I wanted to keep him safe? The calls are worrisome. I was helping out."

"Remember when you were starting out with the tattoo shop?" Cody cocked his head to the side and waited for me to nod. "There were several times you weren't sure you were going to be able to pay the rent to keep it open."

"Yeah, those were tough times." I recalled the first couple years of owning my own business.

"How would you have felt if Micah or I had gone behind your back and paid the rent or convinced the landlord to give you an extension?"

My first answer was partially honest. "I would have been relieved and grateful for the help."

Cody waited, pointedly.

I took a deep breath and then admitted, "And I would have been pissed that you didn't believe in me. I would have felt like a little kid whose parents rushed in to save him instead of letting him make his own way." Running a hand over my face, I sighed. "Damn it, I didn't mean to offend him."

"So, tell him that." Cody shrugged.

"I will." I paused for a sip of coffee. "This whole older younger thing is hard. It's like Jay plays up the Daddy aspect, but I'm not sure how far he wants that to go. I naturally want to take care of him. I see him needing help, and I want to give that help. I want him safe. The calls are worrying me."

"You two need to talk. Open communication is the key to any relationship." Cody sipped his coffee. "I mean, Kennedy and I…" He immediately clamped his mouth shut.

But, it was too late. "You and *Kennedy* what?"

"Nothing." Cody blushed. "I'm saying you and Jay need to talk it out. Is he wanting a Daddy in every sense of the word? Physically, sexually, and emotionally? Discuss your roles. Where are the lines? I think you two are great for each other. I really like Jay, but you have a much better chance of making things work if you're open and honest about your wants, needs, and limits from the very beginning."

"You're right. I'll apologize and we can have a nice long talk." I finished my coffee. "Don't think I'm forgetting about your little slip just now. I bet you've got all kinds of kinky stories to tell, you fucker."

Cody blushed again and laughed. "Maybe."

When I left, I headed to my shop to wait for the one appointment I had that day, which would be at least three hours of work, but the payoff would be great. Before I settled in to work, I texted Jay.

I've got an appointment coming in, but how about dinner at my place tonight? I need to apologize, and we need to talk some things out.

At first, I thought Jay would ignore my request. But, moments before the client walked in, Jay replied.

I'll be there at 6:00.

I spent the next three hours focused on my art and subconsciously making dinner plans. By the time I'd finished the piece and cleaned up the shop, I had over two hours to get home, shower, and have dinner ready.

My heart pounded at the thought of Jay coming over. What was I, some damn horny, head-over-heels high school kid having his first real date? That's what Jay did to me. Annoying little fucker. I smiled at how much I enjoyed being annoyed.

CHAPTER 10

JAY

Once Levi left, I fumed around my humble abode slamming dishes into the dishwasher, slinging wet clothes from the washing machine to the dryer, and pacing in front of my couch. After about an hour, I realized I was doing absolutely nothing but irritating myself even more. I flipped through my phone, pissy that I couldn't even find a song that spoke to me. Fifteen minutes later, after trying to lose myself in music and dance, I finally gave up. I was a mess if I couldn't even find respite in my art.

After a shower and an angry cleaning of my apartment, I jetted from my place and stalked toward Micah's mechanic shop. Before his dad died, the business was Ed's Autos but Micah had recently christened it with a new name and a new sign. Edwards Autos had a gleaming new paint job, glistening new waiting room with comfy chairs, water and coffee for customers, and a small television in the lobby. Micah was working hard to erase the stain of hatred and bigotry his father had left on the shop over the years.

Glancing at my watch, I realized it was lunchtime as I walked past the B & B. But, Levi's truck was there, so I bypassed the place and hoped that Micah's vending machine had some decent choices.

Stepping into the shop, I was surrounded by the scent of rubber, oil, and gasoline.

Randy, a gruff looking, but very friendly bearded man sat behind the front counter. "Howdy. What can I do ya for?"

That type of question from a big bear of a man would have sent me into major flirt mode at one point in my life. But, even as upset as I was with Levi, I could only muster a sincere smile at Randy. "Is Micah in?"

"Yeah, he's in his office with Cole. You want I should let him know you're here?" Randy stood and wiped his hands on his pants.

He was definitely a mechanic. I could tell by the grease stains on his shirt and pants. A sub sandwich sat on the desk so I assumed he was eating lunch while covering for Sadie, Cody's sister. She worked the front counter for extra money between college classes.

"Yeah, would you, please?" I glanced down at Randy's lunch and my damn stomach chose that time to gurgle loudly.

Randy went through the door, and I heard him holler, "Yo, Micah! You got a man here to see ya." When he came back to the front, Randy carried a package. "He said to come on back." Holding the package out to me, Randy blushed. "The sub shop messed up my order. They tried to give me a meat lovers when I ordered a damn veggie sub."

"Nah, I can't take your lunch." I shook my head and held up a hand in protest even though the sandwich sounded fabulous.

"Seriously, I'm a vegetarian. There's no way I'll eat this. The girl behind the counter begged me to take it so the manager didn't know she'd screwed up. I was going to give it to Micah, but Cole brought him lunch. So, it's going to go to waste if you don't take it." Randy offered the sub again.

"Well, when you put it that way. I won't turn down free food." I took the package and nodded toward Randy. "Thanks, man."

"No problem. Glad someone can eat it, hated to see it go bad."

Walking to the back, I found Micah and Cole in the office. "Hey." I sighed and plopped on the couch.

Micah sat behind his desk and Cole sat next to him. They had spread a lunch out between them and seemed to be enjoying their time together. Could have been Levi and me if he hadn't decided to be a jerk. "Sorry to interrupt."

"What's up with you?" Micah squinted and studied me. "Last I heard, Levi was headed to your house with breakfast, hot beverages, and some sort of back washing plan. Why do you now look like someone took a piss in your shoe?"

I frowned at Micah's description of my mood. I crossed my arms like a petulant child who wanted his story heard but wasn't willing to spill it.

"Come on, buddy, you gotta use your words." Cole teased in his best teacher voice.

"Levi did something very not cool. And then he got mad at *me* when he realized I was upset. I kicked him out. I even turned down his offer to wash my back, which itches like a bad case of crabs, might I add, and told him to go home." I winced as I tried to ease the discomfort of my healing skin.

"Whoa, how the hell do you know what crabs feel like?" Micah stopped my rant.

"I mean, it itches like how I'd imagine a bad case of crabs would feel." I was getting crankier by the second. "Don't you even want to know what Levi did?"

"Yeah, I do. Sorry, you threw me off with the crabs." Micah gestured to continue.

"He called Chuck and got me another week off with pay because I got more phone calls." I crossed my arms over my chest and waited for Micah and Cole's outrage.

It didn't come. The men looked confused.

"You're mad because he got you an extra week off with pay? I don't get it." Cole wiped his mouth and took a drink.

"He went behind my back, spoke to my boss, and treated me like a *child*. Not cool." I stressed my annoyance at Levi with each word.

"Did Levi try to hide the fact he called Chuck? Did he lie to you about it?" Micah gathered his trash from lunch and tossed it before relaxing back into his desk chair.

"No, he was upfront about it as soon as Chuck called me." I admitted. "But, the point is, I didn't need him to take care of my mess like I'm some toddler or some little wifey of long ago who can't make decisions or protect myself."

"Sounds like Levi's worried about the phone calls and wants to be sure you're safe. I don't think he's the type to pigeonhole you unless it's one you want." Cole studied me for a moment. "Levi has about a decade more experience than you." When I started to argue, Cole shushed me. "And by that I mean he's been through more. Doesn't mean he knows better or is smarter, just means he's had more years to see things. He cares about you. That much is obvious. He didn't call the school to help me out when I was dealing with all that shit a while back. Levi called Chuck *for you* because he wants to take care *of you*."

"I don't need taken care of!" I bit out.

"Then you two probably need to have a conversation about how far you want the term Daddy to go in your relationship." Micah shrugged.

His words were like ice water on my anger. "What do you mean?"

"Well, is Daddy a term of endearment and a silly little game you play? Or do you want Levi to play more of a daddy role in your life where he's there to guide you, advise you, support you, and comfort you?" Micah leaned forward to rest his elbows on the desk. "Or, do you plan to take it all the way into a deeper meaning of the daddy role and pull in Dom and sub aspects? There's a whole list of Daddy kink you could bring into the relationship."

I started to answer, but the words wouldn't come. I sat, trying to speak, but my mouth just opened and closed several times like a damned dying goldfish.

"Levi doesn't do things randomly and he sure as shit wouldn't have done something if he thought it was going to upset you." Micah's words were soft and gentle, his eyes kind, but I knew he trusted Levi and would die for him. "If anything, he probably thought you'd be thrilled with an extra week off. And, I'm positive his driving motivation was to keep you safe. I bet the fact that you're still getting the phone calls is worrying him and pissing him off big time. Maybe you two need to discuss where things are going to stand with you two. You guys can't go into a new relationship, especially one with such drastic differences, without planning to have a wide-open line of communication."

My anger had been sufficiently drained throughout the conversation. "Wow, I came in here all mad and wanting you to side with me. But, turns out I was actually in the wrong and now I feel like a total ass." My shoulders slumped and I hung my head.

"How did you leave things with Levi?" Cole prompted.

"I mean, I didn't scream and yell and tell him we were over. I told him I needed some time, and I could wash my back by myself." My cheeks heated as I recalled the way I'd reacted to Levi's kind gesture. "Shit, what if he figures I'm going to constantly overreact and behave like a child? I basically proved why our age difference won't work." I ran a hand roughly over my face.

"Nah, Levi probably should have thought his plan through a little more thoroughly and tried to see it from your point of view. He's been on his own for a very long time. He's not used to worrying about others." Micah smiled softly as he spoke of his cousin. "That's probably why the whole daddy thing bothers him so much. He hates it but he also loves it. And he hates that he loves it. But, the thought of having someone to take care of, someone to turn to him, and someone to comfort and support when he's been alone for so long is probably appealing even though he doesn't want it to be."

My heart warmed at the thought of Levi wanting to take care of me. But, the image of Levi all alone made me sad. "Has he never dated?"

"Not really." Micah frowned. "He hooks up. He's had a few guys he's gone out with more than a couple times. But, there's never been that spark." Micah's eyes twinkled. "I think that's why you two have such a connection. Even though Levi wants the world to think you're not his type and you're way too young, he knows you're the first guy to hold his attention longer than a couple weeks. He always went for bigger, burlier guys his age or older, but to no avail. Then Twinky Twinkerbell came along and, no matter how much he tried to fight it, he couldn't."

I smiled at Micah's nickname for me. "Twinky Twinkerbell?"

Micah shrugged and Cole laughed as I preened.

"So, do you think he'll accept an apology?" I worried my bottom lip.

"I'm sure Levi will be willing to have an open conversation. That's one positive to him being older and more experience. He's not as likely to blow up and go off half-cocked." Micah checked his watch. "I've got to get back to the bay to finish up a car and help Randy with three oil changes." He stood and pulled Cole from his chair and wrapped him in a hug. "Thank you for lunch. I'm loving that your lunch and prep period are back-to-back and the school is so close." Dipping his head, Micah kissed Cole. "Love you. See you at home."

"Love you." Cole returned the words and the kiss. "I'll be home if the last two periods today don't kill me. I swear, you'd think some of these kids have never watched a single news program in their lives."

I said goodbye to Cole as he left Micah's office.

"Hey, grab a water on your way out and take this for dessert." Micah tossed me a candy bar. "The machine spit out two earlier when I was getting a snack."

I caught the candy and wrinkled my nose. "Do you all look at me like some loser who can't even afford to buy food? I swear, I appreciate you guys keeping me fed, but I feel like I'm thirteen with no job and having to bum money from friends and parents all the time." I rolled my eyes. "Not that I was ever able to get any money from my parents."

"Nah, we've all been where you were. Starting out is hard. One day you'll be more settled and you can pay it forward to some young guy who needs an extra hand." Micah shrugged. "Now go enjoy your lunch. And talk to Levi."

I nodded. "I will. I'm not sure he's going to want to talk to me."

"He will. I know my cousin. Knowing you're upset is eating at him and he'll want to make it right." Micah slapped me on the back and then winced when I yelped. "Sorry, man, forgot about the ink."

I made a big production of moaning and groaning while walking from the shop as Micah laughed behind me. "How you going to handle round two?" he hollered.

"The actual tattooing wasn't a problem, it's the healing after that hurts and bothers." I shot back. "Tell Randy thanks again for lunch!" I held the sandwich up as I shouldered my way out the front door of the shop.

Micah laughed and waved.

I wandered around BJ for over an hour. It was beyond strange to have so much time on my hands. I loved my job and loved dancing, but I hadn't ever been able to relax and enjoy the town. I moseyed into shops, browsed the merchandise, made mental lists of things I'd love to buy if I ever had extra money, and chatted with local townsfolk. I'd made it to the park when the hair on the back of my neck stood up at the exact moment my phone rang.

It was him. I knew it was. And I had the worst feeling he was nearby.

I accepted the call. "Please stop calling me. I don't want to hurt your feelings, but I'm not interested in you. You're scaring me and I don't like it. Please stop."

Several seconds of silence passed and I awaited the usual hang up. But, instead, I heard hastily whispered words, "I'm sorry," right before the line went dead. The shivery feeling running through my veins disappeared and I felt free. Maybe my words had done nothing in the long run, but for the time being I'd stood up for myself and let the caller know he was making me afraid. I was probably reading into it, but I felt like his words sounded surprised as if he hadn't realized he was creeping me out.

I'd definitely have to tell Levi about the call. If he'd be willing to talk to me.

But, I called Kennedy first and relayed the event to him.

"Maybe you hit a nerve with him. Maybe he really didn't get he was doing anything wrong. The calls may stop. Or, they may ramp up. Either way, keep me updated."

I agreed and hung up. Ambling to the swings, I pocketed my phone and took a seat. How long had it been since I'd played on the swings at the playground? Years and years. I didn't even remember swinging that much as a kid. Pushing off, I used my legs to pump myself higher and higher until I was swinging up so far that I lost my breath with each descending swing. I laughed and flew high until I was almost sick to my stomach. Allowing the swing to slow on its own, I enjoyed the soothing motion and realized I could actually go home and take a nap. When I was a child, naps were used as punishment or to keep me out of the way. As an adult, I very seldom had time for a nap. But, thanks to Levi, I had the freedom to rest and relax for a bit without worrying over bills and budgets.

As I climbed from the swing and headed home, my phone buzzed with a text from Levi.

> *I've got an appointment coming in, but how about dinner at my place tonight? I need to apologize and we need to talk some things out.*

I grinned from ear-to-ear. All but skipping across the playground, I grabbed a drink from the water fountain and paused long enough to send a quick reply.

I'll be there at 6:00.

Then I floated home for a big bowl of cereal and a nap.

My little car puttered up Blueridge Hill toward Levi's house five minutes before six. My afternoon nap had been glorious, and I'd awakened refreshed and ready to fix things. A long, luxurious shower— or as long and luxurious as my hot water heater would allow—and a thick layer of moisturizer on my dry, peeling, itchy back came first. Then I dressed in my favorite red skinny jeans and black t-shirt. Eyeliner and mascara made my eyes pop. With a black blazer and my red and black bowling-style shoes, I was comfortable and knew I looked good.

Levi was sitting on the front porch when I pulled up. His gaze was hot as he watched me exit my car. Once I met his gaze, I couldn't have fought his magnetic pull if I'd tried. I climbed the stairs and walked straight into his arms.

"I'm sorry," we both whispered.

And then I stood and gathered beautiful heat and energy while wrapped in his arms.

"Dinner will be ready in about thirty minutes." Levi let go of me and handed me a bottle of hard cider. "Let's save our more serious talking for after we eat. We can sit out here and enjoy the rest of the evening for a while." He kissed my cheek and led me to the porch swing.

"Thanks." I nodded and gestured with the bottle before taking a long swig. "I need to tell you something."

Levi looked worried, but I watched him gather his emotions quickly. He nodded at me to continue.

"So, I got another phone call today. I was at the park and got a weird vibe, like the kind where the hair stands up on your neck and you're creeped out. Then the phone rang. I answered and told him to please stop calling and that he was scaring me. The call felt different from the others from the very beginning." I paused to take another drink." At first, I thought he was just going to breathe and hang up like usual, but he whispered a shocked and hasty, 'I'm sorry' and then hung up. As soon as he was gone, I felt the weird feeling go away. I don't know if my words did anything or if he'll stop calling, but it felt good to take a stand."

Levi pulled me into his side with an arm around my shoulders. "I'm proud of you. Did you call Kennedy?"

Part of me wanted to huff that I could take care of myself and be trusted with important things, but I paused to remind myself that Levi was concerned and looking out for me. "Yeah, I called and told him all about it. He said the calls may stop or they may ramp up and to keep him updated."

Levi nodded and took a drink from his own bottle.

I snuggled into his side and pulled my legs up on the swing. I sat there in comfortable silence until a buzzer in the house alerted Levi to dinner being ready.

"Come on, let's eat. I'm starving." Levi stood and pulled me from the swing.

Delicious dinner smells filled the air when I walked into the house. "Mmmm, smells so good in here. What did you fix?" I breathed deeply and did my best to keep the drool from dribbling down my chin as I slipped off my shoes.

"Tortilla soup, beef and cheese enchiladas, Spanish rice, and ice cream." Levi listed the foods nonchalantly as he stirred the soup and then pulled the enchiladas from the oven.

"Holy shit. When did you have time to make all of this? And when did you learn to *make* all of this?" I took the plates Levi handed me and set the table. For one brief moment, I had a glimpse of what our evening meals could be like if things between us went well. My heart swelled with anticipation and affection.

"Full disclosure, the soup was from Cody's mom. She stuck it in my freezer for a time when I'd need a quick meal." Levi grabbed two bottles of water and a bottle of wine. Glancing at the label, he shrugged. "The guy at the liquor store promised this was what his wife always wants when they have Mexican for dinner."

I took the bottle and got two glasses. "It's wine. It's fine. But seriously, did you make the rest of the dinner by yourself?"

Levi smirked. "Well, yeah, it wasn't hard. Brown and season some ground beef, wrap it up in a tortilla with cheese, smother it in some enchilada sauce, and bake it. The rice isn't from scratch, but it's pretty darn tasty." Winking, Levi whispered, "The ice cream was going to be flan, but I've never made it and I ran out of time."

"Well, I'm beyond impressed." I kissed Levi's cheek.

I helped bring the meal to the table and then dished it up, filling my plate. Within seconds of my first bite, I fell once again into a comfortable balance of chatter and silence with Levi.

By the time we'd eaten our full, I was trying to think of a way to let Levi know there was no way I could eat ice cream right then, He saved me from gracefully turning down dessert when he spoke. "If you want ice cream, I'll fix it, but I'm going to barf if I eat anything more right now."

Laughing, I agreed. "No, I don't think there's any way I could eat ice cream right now."

"Okay, let's clean up and we can do ice cream later." Levi gathered plates and glasses and carried them toward the sink while I followed with the larger dishes.

"Do you want this packed up for leftovers?" I asked as I eyed the four enchiladas and at least two servings of rice still remaining.

"Yeah, you can take them home. Soup too." Levi tossed me some throwaway plastic containers.

"Just don't heat the food in the plastic. It's not healthy."

I was stuck between being excited for the delicious leftovers and not wanting to appear pathetic, broke, and constantly hungry.

"What's wrong?" Levi's brow crinkled.

Blushing, I stammered, "I don't know. It's hard to decide if I should be grateful for the handout or feel offended that basically the whole damn town knows I can barely feed myself."

"Hey, it's some enchiladas. Don't make it into something bigger than it really is." Levi tipped my chin. "Besides, maybe we'll eat them together for breakfast and you won't have to worry about it." With a gentle brush of his lips on mine, Levi left me wanting more.

"That sounds like a good plan," I muttered before packing up the leftover food. By the time I'd wiped off the counters and the table and put all the extras away, Levi had the dishwasher loaded and the sink emptied.

"Wow, we make a pretty good team in the kitchen." Levi flicked the hand towel toward me.

"Hey, watch it." I jumped from the snapping towel. "Remember, I'm healing an open wound."

Laughing, I followed him into the living room.

Settling down on the couch, Levi took one end and I took the other, but he quickly grabbed my legs and pulled them onto his lap. The perfect set up to talk yet still be connected.

"So, I talked to Cody today and he said we need to work on our communication," Levi began.

"Funny. I talked to Micah and Cole and they said the same thing." Laying my head against the couch's arm, I moaned as Levi rubbed my feet. "God, that feels good."

"I'm sorry for getting you time off without talking to you about it."

Levi's words seemed sincere. "Thank you. I'm sorry for overreacting when all you were trying to do was keep me safe." Just like this gentle massage of my feet, I knew he had been acting out of caring affection when he called Chuck.

"So, there are a lot of things I'd rather be doing than having awkward conversations, but I think it's important we start off things with open communication." Levi rubbed his hands up my calves before turning to face me.

"Agreed." I smiled, dipping my head shyly.

"Okay, first things first." Levi paused until I looked up. "If we do this, it's just us. We're exclusive unless we mutually decide to bring other people in to play."

I nodded. "I didn't wait over two years to fuck around on you. Honestly, I have no interest in adding a third." I hesitated. "Is that something you'd want?"

"Not at all. I tend to have a jealous streak and never really learned to share."

I sighed in relief.

"I gotta put this out there. I'm older, I've seen things, I've done things. Doesn't make me better or smarter, just means I've lived a little longer." Levi ran a hand over his head. "I'll want to protect you, keep you safe, make sure you're okay. It's who I am, it's who I've always been, and especially how I feel toward you."

I crawled across the couch to climb onto Levi's lap. "I will accept your protection and do my best to take it for what it is and not feel like you're seeing me as weak or incapable or pathetic."

Levi's hand cupped the back of my head and pulled me in for a deep kiss.

My lips clung to his as he broke the contact several seconds later.

"You are one of the most beautiful, strong, and amazing people I've ever met. Don't *ever* think differently." Wrapping his arms around me, holding me like a child, he continued. "As far as the *Daddy* stuff. How far are you wanting to take that?"

I laughed at the irony of the question as I sat curled on his lap. "I mean, it started because you're older, and I knew it bugged you. It was my way of getting to you. I know you're going to naturally take the role of a mentor much the way the other guys do because you're all older. I like that. I like having support, advice, and friends to lean on."

"Is that as far as you want it to go?" Levi's fingers played in my hair.

"For now? Yeah. I mean, I'm not against some kinkiness, but I don't see us being all BDSM or anything like that." I pulled back to see his face. "Unless the leather scene that Cody and Kennedy are into is more your thing? Honestly, I'd be willing to try anything with you. But, only with you."

Levi kissed me again. "The leather shit can be sexy as fuck and I wouldn't have any qualms about seeing you in a harness or a cock ring."

At his words, my blood began to boil and I had to concentrate extremely hard to stop thinking about harnesses and cock rings.

"But, I'm not interested in sharing you with others or having sex in front of Cody's customers." Kissing me again, he swirled his tongue against mine. "I have many, many plans for us before I'd get to a point where I wanted to do that."

"I like the sound of that." I kissed him back. "Are we done talking?"

"Let's see, we're keeping our communication open, we'll be faithful, and we'll get as kinky as is mutually comfortable." Levi kissed my lips between each item on the list. "Yeah, I think we've just about talked ourselves out. Should we get ready for bed? I'm tired."

I studied his face, trying to determine if he was serious. "First, you're ready to go to sleep? There's still some light in the sky. Second, am I sleeping over? I didn't bring a bag."

Levi laughed. "When you get in deep with an old man, you've got to be ready for early nights. But, once I get my AARP card, we'll be set. And, think of all the money we can save when I start getting a senior discount."

I slapped his chest. "Stop that. You're older than me, that doesn't mean you're *old.*"

Grabbing my hands between his, Levi kissed them. "As far as number two, I'd like for you to stay if you're comfortable."

Biting my lip, I glanced at him as my cheeks heated. "Are we just going to sleep?"

"That's completely up to you." Levi traced a thumb over my bottom lip. "I definitely won't be fucking you tonight, but I have in mind a ton of other things. But only if you're ready and willing. If not, we'll cuddle up in bed and watch a movie until we both fall asleep and wake up to leftover enchiladas."

"Can we see how things play out? Just let things happen if they happen?" My words were quiet.

"Baby, we can *always* do that. Never think you have to do something you're not totally on board with."

"I mean, having sex with you is all I've wanted for over two years. But, now when I'm faced with the reality of it, it's sort of scaring the shit out of me." I buried my head in his shoulder.

"Speaking of, I'm going to take a shower and make sure things are all good in case we do move that far. You can clean up after me."

Levi's words made me laugh, but I quickly sobered when I realized this was actually happening. Whether we had sex or not, we would be in bed together. There would be kissing and touching.

"Holy shit," I breathed the words in reverence.

"What's wrong?"

"Just realizing, *this* is what it feels like to have a dream come true." Like a little kid experiencing an amazing sight for the first time, I was in complete awe.

"Possible sex with me is a dream come true?" Levi laughed.

"No, a real and true relationship with you is a dream come true. Sex is icing on the cake." The words poured from my heart with one hundred percent honesty.

Levi kissed my nose. "Good answer." Capturing my lips, he devoured my mouth until neither of us had any breath left. "But just know, I plan to make sex with me better than any icing on any cake. Ever."

I could only whimper against his chest.

CHAPTER 11

LEVI

"I'll take the guest shower." I tossed Jay a towel from the hall closet. "There should be supplies in my bathroom cabinets. Feel free to use anything you might need." I winked. "I know I'm going to."

Jay looked at me, confused.

Sighing deeply, I knew he needed it spelled out. "I know you've not had sex, but you're familiar with the preparations that are sometimes needed, right?"

When Jay's cheeks turned bright red, I continued. "Don't be embarrassed. These are things we do for each other and things that should be discussed. Plenty of supplies are in the closet. Use what you want." I leaned over to kiss him. "You can wear some of my clothes to bed. Or none at all. Up to you."

"Okay," Jay squeaked before hurrying to the master bathroom.

My shower was as quick as it could be, considering the things that needed to be done. I wasn't assuming things would lead anywhere tonight, but I wanted to be ready in case. As suspected, Jay's shower took longer. The older, mentor part of me wanted to be in there with him, helping him with the unfamiliar process. But, I also knew that some things were better left private.

When he joined me in the bedroom, his hair still damp and his skin flushed from the warm water, I couldn't help but smile at how innocent and adorable he looked. "How the hell do you look like that and have that flirtatious personality but you've never found a guy you wanted to have sex with?" I tossed him a pair of sweats. "These will be gigantic, but at least you'll be warm."

Jay blushed. "Can I just be warm under *your* blankets?"

Christ.

"Sure." I pulled the covers down and crawled under before patting the mattress in invitation.

Wearing only my boxers, feeling the warmth of Jay's body next to mine, I was positive my brain was going to short circuit. "And you didn't answer my question." I attempted to distract myself.

Jay snuggled up against my chest under the blankets. I felt him shrug. "I don't know. There weren't a lot of gay guys, or at least not a lot of *out* gay guys, where I grew up. And, I was such a 'fairy' according to everyone else that none of the questioning or bi guys wanted to be seen with me. Then I was on my own and trying to survive." Jay tipped up his head to look me in the eye. "And then I met you, and there's been no one else I even thought of wanting to share that with."

Overcome with unexpected emotions, I hugged Jay close and kissed the top of his head. Was I getting into this way too quickly? "Can I ask a question?" I hoped to maybe alleviate some of the seriousness.

Jay nodded.

"Your apartment can't cost much. Your car payment and insurance can't be eating up all of your money. You are hungry all the time, but I don't think you're spending all your income on food." I stroked his back, loving the shiver that went through him. "Where does all your money go?"

Jay tensed in my arms.

"Hey, it's okay. You don't have to tell me. I'm sorry. I was being nosey." I tipped his chin and kissed him softly.

"No, it's okay. I didn't realize anyone had noticed I should have more money at my disposal." Jay shifted and ran his hand along my chest, leaving a fiery trail of longing with each trace of his fingers. "So, you and others probably won't get it, and I don't even completely understand it myself, but it is what it is."

I silently chastised myself for getting more and more turned on by the second while Jay was preparing to tell me something that sounded pretty significant. "It's okay, you can tell me anything."

"So, you know how I told you my dad left and my mom is an addict, right?" Jay reminded me of the story he'd told of his shitty childhood.

I nodded.

"Well, as much as I hated living in that town and having a mom who was either high or passed out or not involved, I've always felt a sense of guilt over leaving."

"What? Why?" I immediately wanted to defend him and protect him from his thoughts, but I gathered myself and stopped. "Sorry, go on."

"A little voice inside my head constantly reminds me that my dad left and then I did the exact same thing. Part of me feels like I should have stayed and taken care of her. Or forced her into rehab. Or something." Jay sighed.

"Baby, she neglected you. She all but abandoned you. You owe her nothing." I had to speak up. I couldn't stand to hear Jay feeling guilty over saving himself from a bad situation. "So, where is your money going?" I was pretty sure I knew the answer.

"Likely to feed Mom's addiction, but I tell myself it's going to take care of her."

"I can't believe she lets you send her money and leaves you barely surviving month to month." I gritted my teeth in an effort to calm myself. "She thought only of herself when you were little, and she's still letting you suffer so she can have what she wants and needs."

Jay shifted again. "Um, she doesn't know I'm sending the money."

"Who does she think it's coming from?" I scoffed.

"I don't think she cares. As long as she can get her next bottle of pills or bottle of wine, she doesn't question things." Jay shrugged.

"You have to do what you feel is best, but not a single person would blame you if you stopped sending her money." I did my best to keep the anger from my voice. "You owe her *nothing*."

"I owe her my life," Jay whispered.

"She gave birth to you, but other than that, what did she do? Left a small child to fend for himself, wasn't around to support you, and made your life so hellish that leaving town and living paycheck to paycheck was a better option than living with her." I moved so I could look directly at him. "Again, you owe her nothing."

"I mean, I get by all right," Jay muttered.

"You should at least start sending a little less each time. We can work out a budget so you can keep your fridge and pantry stocked first and foremost. Then you can send her what you feel is right. And slowly wean down to next to nothing." I kissed him hard and fast. "You are a grown man. A strong, resilient, amazing man. You are who you are because of your experiences and your mom is part of that. But, that doesn't mean you need to keep suffering because of her."

"I'm willing to work on it." Jay snuggled back into my arms. "Having money to keep food around would be really nice." He was silent for several moments. "Thanks. You're the first person I've ever told that story, and I think hearing you say I don't owe her anything was something I really needed. Like I couldn't give myself permission to leave her hanging, but having someone else say it feels good."

I thought through his words. "I'm glad you feel that way. But, don't ever rely on me or anyone else to give you permission to do what's best. You are your own person, you have to believe that and trust yourself."

Jay nodded.

We sat in comfortable silence for about five minutes.

"Hey," Jay whispered.

"Yeah?"

"If we were to do anything sexual tonight, what do you think it might be?" He glanced up at me, biting his lip.

I drew in a deep breath. Was I seriously prepared for guiding a virgin through all the intimate intricacies of sex without busting a nut five minutes into everything? "First things first, protection is always a must. Always."

Jay nodded.

"I'm serious. You use condoms every single time. Even if the guy swears up and down he's clean. Even if he has some flimsy piece of paper from a supposed clinic or doctor. Unless you see the test results handed to him, don't take his word for it. You'll end up pissing blood and begging for antibiotics. Protection. Always." How many horny men had believed their partner was clean only to end up with some infection?

"What about you?" Jay traced his finger over my nipple, and I clenched my teeth as it pebbled under his touch.

"What about me?"

"Are you clean?"

"Yes, but we'll go to the clinic together and get tested. Protection always unless you're one thousand percent confident in your partner's sexual health." I knew I sounded like a total prude, but I didn't want Jay to get himself in trouble.

"You'd do that for me?"

Leaning in to kiss him softly, I whispered, "I'm beginning to think there's very few things I wouldn't do for you."

Jay's eyes shimmered and he launched himself at me, continuing the kiss I'd started.

"So, protection is a must," Jay prompted. "After establishing that fact, what else do you think could possibly happen tonight?"

"That would depend on what you're comfortable with." I nipped at his lip. "We can do as much or as little as you want." I paused for a brief moment. "But, I won't be fucking you."

Jay frowned. "Why? You said as little or as much as I want. What if I want that?"

"Believe me, I want that, too. But, not tonight." I scooted to lie down on the bed rather than propped up against the headboard.

Jay joined me, and we faced each other on our sides.

Every ounce of my being fought the urge to grab his ass and rut my hard cock against his until we both came all over ourselves. "Tonight will be a night of firsts for you, but it won't be your first time to bottom. We'll work our way up to that. I want you to experience it all. And you'll start by experimenting on me so you can feel exactly how fucking amazing it will be when I finally do top you."

"Jesus, if you keep talking like that I'm going to embarrass myself before we even get started." Jay groaned.

"You and me both, kid. You and me both." I laughed and pulled him close for a kiss.

Our lips met at the exact moment our chests and hips came together, and I knew then and there that I'd never felt anything so perfect and so right. Everything my past hookups had been lacking was now pressed between our hot bodies and warm hearts, and I never wanted to lose it. "Fuck, that's so good," I mumbled against his mouth as our bodies rocked together.

"I think I'd like a bedtime story." Jay grinned wickedly as he thrust his hips into mine, our cocks already leaking as they strained to make contact through the fabric of my boxers.

I laughed at the absurd statement. "A bedtime story? About what?" My head wasn't exactly in story telling mode.

"About what sexy-as-sin Daddy plans to do with his twinky little boy." Jay bit his lip to keep from laughing.

"Ah, that type of story, huh?" The kid wanted to play? I could play. "It just so happens that I have the perfect story for you."

"Yeah?"

"Mmhm," I whispered against his mouth. "Now hush and listen."

Jay's eyes never left mine as he nodded his agreement.

"Well, the very distinguished older gentleman has had sexy as fuck dreams about what he wants to do to his little boy toy." I began the story and prayed I could make it through without coming in my pants.

"You're not that old," Jay protested.

"Hush, who's telling this story?" I nipped at his lip and swiped my tongue over it to relieve the sting. "So, the more mature man wants nothing more than to swallow his boy's cock until he gags on it."

Jay closed his eyes and moaned.

I allowed my eyes to close. I wanted to hear and feel every single part of Jay as I told this story. "I'm going to suck you deep before I move to trace my tongue along your balls. When you think you can't take any more, I'm going to eat your ass. My tongue slowly rimming your tight virgin hole."

"Jesus fuck, Levi," Jay panted and reached for his cock.

At Jay's movement, I opened my eyes and batted away his hand. "No touching."

Jay whimpered, but kept his eyes closed. "Go on."

"When your balls draw up so tight it's almost painful, I'm going to stop tonguing your ass," I whispered.

"What? Why?" Anguish filled his strangled words.

"Because then it will be your turn to suck me." I cupped his ass. "I'll feed you my dick slowly so I can watch that beautiful pink mouth take every single inch."

"You gotta stop," Jay gasped and ground his cock into mine.

"Nah, we're just getting to the good part," I teased his lips with my tongue before brushing soft kisses against his lashes. "I'll roll to my back so I can see every bit of that gorgeous body. You'll line your cock up with my ass and slide in slowly as I press against the burn of you filling me."

"Stop, you have to stop. I can't do this much longer," Jay groaned and grabbed the base of his shaft, squeezing hard.

"You interested in making this story less fictional?" I nuzzled his neck.

"Fuck yeah." Jay's words escaped in a ragged whisper.

"Then fuck my mouth, baby."

Arms, legs, and dicks tangled and repositioned for a few awkward moments, but I eventually found my face level with the most stunning cock I'd ever seen. Long like the rest of Jay, but not nearly as lean as I had been expecting. "Damn, you've been hiding the goods," I teased before licking his tip.

Jay hissed. "The goods have been here the whole time, you just weren't interested in browsing. Ahh, fuck."

Swallowing down Jay's impressive length, I skipped pumping his shaft to move right to the next part of the story. Trailing my tongue down to lick his balls, I slowly sucked each into my mouth before continuing to his ass. Parting him, I teased first with a spit-slick finger and then with the tip of my tongue. Licking Jay's most sensitive area, I paused to add to the tale. "Someday, I'll work you open with my finger and tongue and then fill this pretty little ass with my big, fat dick."

Jay moved with lightning speed rolling me to my back and straddling my hips. "This story needs to fast forward before I come all over myself." He worked my boxers down and followed with his mouth until he could swirl his tongue around the leaking tip of my pulsing cock. "We'll have to work on a more drawn out story at another time, I need to reach the climax of this plot *now*."

I laughed at his literal and figurative innuendo as I grabbed the lube from the bedside table. Sheathing Jay's cock in latex first, I shared the lube with him before slicking my own ass.

"Levi, I don't have a single fucking clue what I'm doing here," Jay muttered.

"Does your cock feel like it's about to explode?"

"Hell yes."

"Do you feel like you're going to die if you don't get to slide into something hot and tight?" I had to grip my dick to keep from blowing with each word.

Jay whimpered and nodded as he fingered my ass.

"Then fuck me, baby. Slide that gorgeous cock deep in my ass and make me come all over myself." I lifted my legs and opened my body to him.

Never had I seen anything more beautiful and mesmerizing than Jay lining up his dick and inching slowly into my body. The sting was breathtaking, and I panted as my body adjusted. "God, yes, Jay. Now just do what feels best." *And please let that be thrusting deep into my ass over and over.*

Jay's gaze rested on his cock pumping in and out of my body for several moments. "Never wanted to top, but this is amazing."

"Yeah? You can top me anytime you want." I jacked myself as my balls drew up.

"Hell no. I'm so damn jealous of you right now. I can't wait to be where you are." Jay increased his depth and speed.

I choked on a laugh. "Why's that?" *Stupid question* I thought as my body electrified from the inside out with each stroke of his length.

"Because I want my Daddy's big, fat cock deep in my ass." Jay bit his lip and pumped harder and faster.

Those last words did me in and I shot all over my stomach.

"Fuuuuuck, that's fuckin' amazing," Jay groaned. With a final, deep thrust, he spilled into the condom, cock pulsing. "Oh my god," he panted. "That was the most intense, amazing thing ever."

Careful not to be too rough with his back, I pulled him forward to kiss him thoroughly. "Yes, yes it was. And wait until you've got my cock drilling your ass while you shoot your load."

Jay shifted and pulled from me gently.

We both winced at the loss of our most intimate contact.

"We need another shower," he mumbled but rolled to his side and cuddled against me.

"A towel will be fine for now." I moved to the side of the bed and reached for the towel I'd left on the floor. Wiping us both off, I tossed the cloth back to the ground and gathered Jay in my arms. Kissing the top of his head, I held him tight. "How'd you like that story?"

"Best damn story I've ever heard. I liked the live action event even more." Jay snuggled into my chest. "I'm really looking forward to the sequel. I hear the characters are going to switch up their roles which promises to be a real show stopper." Jay giggled sleepily at his own joke.

Within moments, I fell asleep in his arms.

~*~*~

We slept through the night, only waking slightly to reposition and adjust our tangled arms and legs. When the sun trickled through the blinds and a rooster at the bottom of Blueridge Hill crowed, Jay began to stir. Throughout the night, he had tried his best to play little spoon to my big spoon, but I didn't want my bare chest plastered against his still healing skin. So I kept him snuggled chest-to-chest. When the earliest train whistle blasted through BJ, Jay finally awakened enough to speak.

"Morning," he whispered but kept his head tucked.

"Good morning." I tipped his chin and forced his beautiful eyes to look at mine. "Sleep okay?"

He nodded. "Honestly, best night of sleep I've had in years." Jay blushed before kissing me. "So, thank you."

I continued the kiss before pulling away to smile at Jay's gorgeous sleep-mussed hair. "My pleasure. Let me take a look at your back. Probably can do the rest of the tattoo in the next day or so."

When he turned over, I studied my work, pleased with the design. "Yeah, this looks good. We can move on as early as tomorrow."

"Was it okay? I mean, was *I* okay?"

Jay's insecurities, so well camouflaged behind his big personality and makeup and bright colors, came bubbling to the surface. Cupping his chin, I kissed him before offering assurance. "Baby, last night was beyond wonderful and perfect and amazing. You were breathtaking. My only regret is that I'm too sore to have a repeat performance this morning."

Jay's face contorted in a mixture of pride and pouting. "I was hoping for at least a slight replay."

"A *slight* replay is definitely doable." I kissed him, sliding my tongue against his and imagining what it would be like to wake up with this man in my bed every morning.

CHAPTER 12

JAY

I was living in a dream world. That was the only explanation. If it truly was a dream, I never wanted to wake up. After lusting over Levi and following him around for years, he'd finally taken notice. Or, more accurately, he'd finally admitted he couldn't fight the attraction between us. Even though I'd longed for Levi to see me as more than just an annoying kid during the past couple years, I was actually glad he'd taken so long to come around. We were friends first, even though I bugged the hell out of him. As much as I'd wanted things to happen faster, I'm not sure I would have been ready for that. Maybe I was getting more mature and all that shit.

Good things come to those who wait.

I smiled as I climbed into my car. Heading toward Levi's shop, I was giddy with excitement and anticipation. Sex with Levi had been amazing, and I could barely think of anything else. My tattoo was stunning and I knew it would be exquisite by the time Levi finished his work of art. I loved my time off because I got to spend more time relaxing with Levi, but I was also looking forward to getting back to work. I missed dancing. And I was going to take a big step in sending less money to my mother each month.

I gathered my jumble of random thoughts as I pulled into a spot at the back of Levi's shop. Recalling how he had told me I could park next to his truck instead of out front like all the other customers brought a big goofy grin to my face, and I bounded from the car. Swinging open the back door to the shop, I immediately felt a sense of calm come over me when bombarded by the scent of ink and antiseptic. Listening for a moment, I waited until my eyes had adjusted to the dimmer indoor lighting and heard Levi's gun buzzing in one of the rooms.

Not wanting to interrupt Levi's session, I took a trip to the bathroom and then helped myself to an energy drink from the fridge in his office.

"That you, Jay?" Levi called out when the buzz of the gun paused.

I smiled, happy to think he'd stop his work to check on me. "Yeah, I'm a little early." I rounded the corner of the doorway to find Levi working over a piece on a man's arm. A beautiful, gorgeous, breathtaking piece on an arm as big as one of my thighs. Not to mention a man as impressively attractive and fit as any sports model I'd ever seen. Instantly feeling scrawny and twinkish, I started to slink back toward the door. My heart hurt, I hadn't run from who I was in the years since leaving my hometown, but I didn't want to bring problems for Levi.

"Hey, don't go. I'm almost done here," Levi called out.

Unsure what Levi wanted, I walked back into the room.

The man under the gun gazed at me with hungry eyes.

"Nico, this is my…," Levi paused and glanced at me with panic-stricken eyes.

I made a face and shrugged to let him know he was on his own. Did I want him to introduce me as his boyfriend? Hell yeah. But, I didn't want him to feel pressured, so I stayed neutral.

Levi cleared his throat. "Um, this is my boyfriend, Jay."

My world froze and my heart stopped beating for a few seconds. *Boyfriend.* Was I really Levi's boyfriend? Or had he said the word to protect me from Nico who looked like he wanted to eat me alive?

"Pretty," Nico grunted.

"Not available," Levi growled back before he started the gun again.

Definitely just to protect me. That was okay. We could work up to Levi meaning the word boyfriend.

"You should bring him to Cody's sometime," Nico suggested.

"Maybe," Levi spoke above the noise of his needle.

I appreciated Levi's uninterested answer.

"He like to play?"

Nico clearly wasn't letting his suggestion go.

"We like to play *together*. That's it." Levi tossed a worried glance my way.

"Levi is plenty for me to play with, definitely no worries there," I quipped and then winked at my man.

"If you ever want to share the fun, you know where to find me."

Nico's words were low and meant to be seductive but only came across as creepy.

"Yeah, I do, but don't hold your breath," Levi mumbled as he wiped ink and blood from Nico's arm.

"Damn, Wells, I'm just sayin'. You used to like to play. You going all boring vanilla on us now?" Nico's question held a challenge.

Shit. Was that what Levi wanted? What he needed? I wasn't against getting kinky, but I sure didn't have experience in that department.

Levi laid the gun on the table and began to clean Nico's arm. "Nah, just no need for the props and extras when I've got all the man I need right in my own bed."

My heart filled with warm relief.

Nico huffed but shut his mouth while Levi finished covering up his new ink.

"You know the routine." Levi taped down the final corner of the bandage. "Keep it clean, keep the ointment on it, and call me if it gets red or infected."

Nico stood and nodded at Levi. "Will do." Turning toward the door, Nico trailed his eyes up and down my body. "You ever find you need a bigger, better daddy, you look me up, hear?"

Cocking out a hip and gathering as much sass as I could muster, I batted my lashes, glad I'd worn the sparkly mascara, and pursed my lips. "I've got *all* the daddy I need. I'm definitely not left wanting nor am I looking."

Nico frowned but nodded before walking from the room.

When the front door of the shop rang with Nico's exit, I finally let out the breath I'd been holding.

Levi gathered me in his arms. "I'm so sorry." He led me from the room and into his office. "I didn't think Nico would come on to you like a complete asshole. Again, I'm sorry. You okay?" He sat me down on the couch and then went to wash his hands.

"I'm fine. Who is he? Did you two date?" I wasn't sure I truly wanted to know the answer, but I couldn't help myself.

"Date? No." Levi shook his head and walked back to the couch. As he dropped to a cushion, he pulled me onto his lap. "The few times Cody has talked me into more than just casual observing at the B & B Nico has been there and we've played a bit."

My heart sank and I immediately felt inferior and way out of Nico's league. "So, that's the type you like? That's what you mean when you say I'm not your type?" I truly didn't mean to sound pathetic and pouty, but I felt the words came out that way.

"No, that's not what I said." Levi hugged me close and kissed my neck before tipping my chin so he could have my mouth. "Nico is a Neanderthal mostly. Fun to play with maybe, but no connection, no spark."

"But, you had sex with him?"

"Baby, I'm a gay man in my thirties, I've had sex with several guys. Doesn't mean I'm into them, doesn't mean I'm going to date them, doesn't mean I fell in love with them and want to settle down." Levi kissed me again. "I can't change my past any more than you can change yours. But, I can assure you, as I told you earlier, if we're doing this, it'll be exclusive. If at some point you want something added to our relationship, that's open for discussion. Until then, it's you and me and no one else."

Hearing the words warmed my heart, but thinking about Nico's strong physical presence still had me worried. "Did you bottom for him like you did for me?"

"No. You're the first person I've bottomed for in many, many years."

I glanced up at him. "Really?"

Levi smiled, "Yes, really."

"He's so big and muscular and tough looking. How could you go from guys like that to me?" I wasn't fishing for compliments, just not feeling very confident.

"I'm beginning to think all the guys I found attractive and spent any time with sexually were the exact opposite of 'my type.' In fact, I'm beginning to think that this whole 'my type' thing is a big farce. I can't stop thinking about your sleek, slim body. The way I can wrap you in my arms and hold you safe and protected. A stark contrast does exist between us, but the way our bodies match and fit is such an odd yet beautiful pairing." Levi paused and shook his head. "Does that even make sense? I feel like a crazy person talking right now." He kissed me, making love to my mouth before cupping my face with his hands. "I don't even see those other guys now, all I see is you."

"That's nice to hear." I bit my lip, uncertain about what I wanted to say.

"What is it? What's wrong?" Levi reached for my hand.

"You introduced me as your boyfriend. Was that to protect me from Nico's come-ons?" I blushed.

"Partly." Levi smiled. "I will say it was a little awkward. I wasn't exactly sure how to introduce you. But, when I saw Nico look at you the way he did, I figured using boyfriend was better. If it upset you, I knew I could apologize to you later."

"It didn't. But, I didn't want you to think you had to use it or that you have to keep using it now that you've said it once. I mean, I get that it was to keep Nico from hitting on me."

"Not that it worked terribly well." Levi laughed. "Can you imagine how hard he would have pressed if I'd introduced you as a friend?"

"Yeah, he was pretty intimidating."

Levi tipped my chin again. "But, I didn't call you my boyfriend just to save you from Nico."

"No?" My heart pounded and tried to climb into my throat.

"No." Levi kissed my eyelids, my cheeks, and my lips. "I like the sound of the word."

"How did we go from me being an annoying frustration and you staunchly denying you found me even the least bit attractive to having sex in your bed, making out in your office, and you introducing me as your boyfriend?" I pulled back to look at Levi. "I mean, seriously, is this a dream, and I'll be crushed when I finally wake up?"

Levi laughed. "If it's a dream, I'm in the same one. And hell if I know what happened between us.

Maybe you finally just wore down my defenses. Maybe you finally got inside the shields and got your hands on my heart. Whatever happened, I'm sorry it took me two years to finally admit I couldn't keep fighting it."

"Don't be sorry." I shook my head. "I was thinking about it on the way here. If you'd taken me up on all my offers, I don't think we'd be here today. Neither of us were ready. I was way too young and had no clue what I was doing. I was still hurting from my past. I'm glad it took us this long. I feel like what we have now could actually turn into something. Two years ago, I the lust and longing may have worn off way too quickly, and we would have just gone our separate ways."

Levi seemed to think about my words for a while. "You're probably right. Two years of getting to know you, even when you were driving me insane, was probably better for us in the long run than a few quick hookups."

I sat in comfortable silence for several moments. It was good to talk things out with Levi.

"You want to start the rest of your tattoo?"

Levi's words came across soft and sleepy.

"Mmm, I don't know, this feels really good." I hummed against his chest as he held me close.

"Want to lock my office door and fuck around for a while *then* finish your tattoo?" Levi whispered in my ear.

I jerked up to look at him. "Can we *do* that?"

"I'm the boss. We can do whatever the hell we want." Levi moved me from his lap. "I'm going to lock the front and put the Closed sign out."

My body shivered in anticipation as I watched him leave the room.

When Levi returned, he shut the door to his office and turned the lock.

His gaze never leaving mine, Levi moved to the couch and pulled me up from my seat. His arms held me tight and his mouth devoured mine. "Dance for me."

"A whole dance like I'd do on stage? Or like a lap dance?" My cheeks burned and my heart pounded in anticipation.

"Whatever gets you naked the quickest," Levi growled.

"Well, regular customers don't get to see me completely naked. Ever." I shimmied my hips against his. "But, for my special daddy customers, I can make an exception and take things to the next level." I traced the shell of his ear with my tongue.

"There better only be one special daddy customer getting that exception." Levi's hands gripped my ass and picked me up so I could wrap my legs around his waist. "God, baby, I can't even imagine how good it's going to be the day I get to take this gorgeous ass of yours."

"That day could be today."

"Not yet. And not in my office."

I pouted.

"But that doesn't mean we can't have a little fun." Levi released me, letting my body slide down his. "Dance for me."

"You get naked first."

Levi narrowed his eyes.

"It's part of the Daddy package. You get naked so I can watch how turned on you are while I strip and dance for you." I bit my lip and waited for Levi to obey. When he stood and began to strip, I felt a sharp zing of hot power shot through me. This man, this gorgeous, stubborn, wonderful man was stripping to his most vulnerable all because I asked him to and because he wanted to see me naked, as well.

His shoes were first, then his shirt hit the floor, followed quickly by his socks and pants. His beautiful cock was straining against his boxer briefs. With his gaze never leaving mine, Levi eased the briefs slowly down his hips, springing his erection free to slap his stomach.

I stepped forward, planning to drop to my knees and worship him.

Levi stopped me. "Nope, I followed directions. Now it's your turn."

With a sly smile, I pressed at his chest until he sat on the couch. While a song played in my mind, I started a slow and sultry strip tease. I worked my tank over my head in increments, toeing off my shoes then my socks. With only my capri length sweatpants dangling precariously from my hips, I began a lap dance sure to have Levi busting a nut sooner rather than later.

Levi's hands caught my waist, his thumbs hooking into my sweats. "Off."

I smirked and shook my head. "No touching the dancers."

"The Daddy package gets exceptions, remember." Levi hauled me by my shoulders to his chest and kissed me with such fire and passion I wanted to end the game right then and there and get to the main event.

"Fuck, Levi."

As if reading my mind, Levi pushed me away and smiled his own sly smile. "Nope, I wanted a dance and dance is what I'm going to get."

Determined to make him suffer in the best way possible, I returned to my standing position and continued to rock and sway to the music in my head. My cock was throbbing, impossibly hard, and I longed to take Levi's shaft in my mouth, to taste him, to tongue his head, to nestle my nose against his balls. But, Levi wanted a dance so I'd give him a dance.

Shimmying my pants down until they pooled around my ankles, I gracefully stepped from them and used a toe to toss them Levi's direction. Knowing the sexy jock I'd chosen that morning would give Levi a definite eye full, I danced a one-eighty so my ass was right at Levi's eye level. A few shimmies, some shakes, and a quick twerk should have ended things, but Levi held out. Standing with my back to him, I tossed a glance over my shoulder and nearly shot my load to find Levi stroking his cock and watching me with a raging fire in his eyes. Reaching down to grab my ankles, I took a quick look at Levi and knew he was about ready to give up the fight. Facing him first, I stalked a few steps closer. I straddled his lap and dropped my balls right onto his cock. "Still want that dance?"

"Fuck, no." Levi grabbed the back of my head and pulled me into a ferocious kiss, a kiss that tasted of longing and desire and lust. But there was more, there was promise and caring and a future. After pushing me to the soft rug on the floor, Levi turned me onto my stomach. "Face down, ass up, baby."

Knowing Levi had said no full-on sex yet, I was unsure what to expect. When his hands parted my ass and his hot, probing tongue rimmed my hole, I fought to keep my legs from giving out beneath me. "Fuuuuuck, Levi."

"Good?" He continued to tongue fuck my ass as he reached around to grip my cock.

I could only pant and press my ass back for more of his tongue. Levi gently teased my hole with a spit-wet finger before entering me a tiny bit with a press of his digit.

"Damn, baby. You're so fucking tight." Levi continued to work his slick finger into my ass. "Can't wait until I'm right here and can fill this beautiful ass with my cock."

With Levi's hand pumping my dick, his tongue and finger teasing my hole while his words fucked with my mind, I couldn't fight the raging orgasm that slammed through me. Once I'd erupted all over Levi's fist, I moved to my knees to take his cock in my mouth.

"Fuck, baby boy. Look at those damn pretty lips sucking my dick deep. Yeah, take it all, baby." Levi thrust into my mouth.

His words, his scent, and his taste all made my cock grow heavy again. With one hand teasing his balls and the other playing with his hole, I sucked his cock deep, stroking it with my tongue.

"Jay, baby, I'm going to come."

I pulled off long enough to pant, "I want your come, Daddy." And took him back in my mouth in time for him to lose himself and shoot his load straight down my throat. I swallowed hard and lapped at his slit as he continued to pulse his release.

Levi dropped to his knees and took me in his arms. Kissing me, dipping his come stained fingers into my mouth, and pressing our throbbing cocks together, he moved us to our sides on his office rug. With our bodies touching from head to toe, Levi held me in his arms as we both caught our breath. "Jay Owens, you have completely ruined me for anyone else ever again. That was fucking amazing." He kissed me. "You're amazing."

"It was pretty damn fabulous, huh?" I smiled. "And ruining you for anyone else ever again was all part of my evil plan."

"We really should clean up and get your tattoo finished, but laying here until we can get it up for round two sounds so damn good." Levi's words came across low and relaxed.

"Let's get the ink done. I'm dying to see the rest of it." I wiggled my hips against his, loving the little stirring I felt in both our dicks. "And round two can continue tonight. Maybe even round three and four."

Levi groaned. "Damn, baby. Ae you sure you want to get involved with an older guy? I may not be able to keep up. You're like a damn little Energizer bunny."

"Being with me will keep you young and fit. Just think of our sex life as being fulfilling for your mind, your body, *and* your heart." I teased as I rolled him to his back. Straddling his hips, I positioned myself so his softened cock was against my hole. "Soon, very soon, you're going to top me." I placed my hands against his chest. "That big, fat, beautiful cock of yours will ease into my ass and you will ruin me for anyone else ever again. My ass *will* belong to you and only you."

Levi groaned. "Fuuuuck, Jay, keep talking like that, and I'll forget about being all noble and caring and I'll take you right here."

My ears perked up. "Really?"

"No, not really. The first time I have your ass won't be on my office floor." He thrust up his hips. "Now, let's get ourselves cleaned up and get this damn fine piece of artwork finished."

CHAPTER 13

LEVI

"I swear I'm not sure I've ever had someone get as blissed out as you during a tat." I kept my words soft, speaking just loud enough to be heard over the gun's buzz.

"It hurts a little more this time, especially in the parts where it's still healing." I paused to wipe his skin and Jay shifted on the seat. "But, it's like once I get past the initial pain it's a good hurt, almost hypnotic." My gun went over his shoulder blade and Jay sucked in a sharp breath. "Except when you hit areas like that."

"Sorry, over bone is always the worst." I sat back and studied Jay's skin. Over the last hour, I'd added highlights and lowlight, shadows and shading, and the final touches to the design. While the image I'd created was magnificent, I knew I'd saved the crowning touch for last.

Fragile strength.

In a font specifically chosen to portray a delicate boldness, I inked the text into Jay's skin. I cleaned and wiped Jay's back. "Want to see it before I smear the ointment all over?"

"Duh." Jay tossed a grin over his shoulder.

"Here, I think a mirror will give you the best view." I gave him a mirror and turned him so his back was to the large reflection on the wall. "I still want to take a picture, but you'll get a better view of it this way."

Jay shifted and repositioned the hand-mirror for several moments before settling on what he must have deemed a good angle.

The silence was deafening.

Was he still breathing?

And then I saw the shimmer of tears in his eyes.

"You hate it?" I always worried that a client wouldn't like my artistic interpretation of their vision.

"Shut up, you dork," Jay choked on a sob. "It's the most beautiful piece of work I've ever seen."

My cheeks heated and I smiled. "I had the most beautiful canvas to work on."

"It's like I can actually see the tiny little droplets of dew sparkling in the morning sun. The whole web almost shimmers." Jay continued to gaze at his back through the mirror. "Where did you even get the idea for this?"

I shrugged. "I was thinking about how fragile you appear in some ways, how innocent you are, and how that contrasts with your strength and resiliency. *Fragile strength* came to mind. I thought about things that are delicate and fragile yet strong and resilient and came up with the spider web."

Jay dropped the mirror onto the chair and threw his arms around my neck. "Thank you," he whispered. "It's the most gorgeous tattoo I've ever seen and the fact that you made it especially for me makes it all the more special. I've never seen something so perfectly me." Jay kissed my neck, my earlobe, my jawline, and finally my lips.

While I kept from rubbing against his back, I grabbed his hips and pulled him close. "And I've never worked on a piece of ink I'm so personally attached to and proud of. Thank you for being my inspiration."

I finished in the shop about thirty minutes later, and I walked with Jay to the back door. "Want to come to my place? I'll make something to eat." I nodded toward Blueridge Hill.

"Can we have the guys over and build a bonfire?"

"Sure, sounds like a great idea." I pulled my phone from my pocket. "You want to grab a bag at your place first?"

"Yeah, probably should. Your clothes definitely don't fit me, and I can't lounge around naked the whole time."

"Wouldn't bother me." I winked.

"I should at least have something to wear in case we go to town. Let me run home for a bag, and I'll be at your house about ten minutes behind you." Jay kissed my cheek.

"I'll invite the guys over." I thumbed a group text to the BJ Boys before I watched Jay's little car putter away from the shop.

All the guys replied in the affirmative before I even pulled out of the shop's parking lot. On my drive up the hill, I couldn't wipe the smile from my face. Who knew having a boyfriend would be so fucking awesome?

By the time I reached the house, Cody had already pulled in the drive. Micah was driving Cole down the hill from their new house. And Kennedy pulled in right behind me.

"Damn, great timing. Were you all hanging around waiting for an invite? Don't you have lives of your own?" My words were met with laughter.

"Well, someone's in a good mood," Micah teased.

"Mmhm, could it be that *someone* is getting some from a certain queen we all know and love?" Kennedy's voice lilted with the ribbing question.

"A true gentleman doesn't kiss and tell." I placed my hand against my chest with a dramatic flair I could have only learned from Jay.

"Where is our little princess?" Cody turned to look down the driveway.

"He ran home to pick up a few things." I shrugged. "Should be here in about ten minutes."

Twenty minutes later, we had the fire built and burning, hamburgers and hotdogs sizzling on the grill, and beer flowing. But, Jay hadn't arrived.

The shrill whistle of a passing train sent a shiver down my spine. Was something wrong? Jay wouldn't have decided not to come without telling me. He was too excited about the evening.

Was he missing because of the phone calls? Did he get another one?

I forced myself to wait two more minutes before I dialed his number. With each ring, I worried my heart would stop beating. Finally, I heard the crunch of gravel on the drive as Jay answered.

"Awww, Daddy, were you missing me?" Jay purred. He climbed from his car with the phone held to his ear before walking toward me.

"Everything okay?" I frowned, still worried because something seemed off. Frowning deeper when I realized I was speaking into the phone while Jay now stood right in front of me, I huffed and ended the call with a roll of my eyes. "Seriously, you okay?"

Jay smiled. "All's good. Just got caught up admiring my new ink."

I had no reason to *not* believe him, but for some reason I knew Jay was hiding something. Grabbing his hand before he was able to join our group of friends, I whispered gruffly in his ear. "I don't know why you're lying, but you'll tell me about it later. You hear?"

Jay quickly nodded. "Yeah. But, later."

Though troubled, I went inside and threw his bag in my room then came back out to find Jay in the middle of showing off his new ink.

"Damn, man, that's amazing." Micah whistled.

Cole nodded in apparent agreement. "Definitely makes me want to have you ink me, Levi."

"*Fragile strength*, it's absolutely perfect." Cody moved Jay into better lighting and studied the tattoo more closely.

"Like you know anything about being fragile," Kennedy scoffed under his breath.

His words were so low I wasn't sure if he *meant* for them to be heard or if anyone had actually heard them.

"Shut up. Like you'd know anything about strength," Cody shot back.

Clearly, Cody *had* heard.

Within seconds, the two men were chest to chest, staring each other down. Kennedy had the advantage in height, but Cody took the lead easily in sheer brawn.

"Just because I look big and bad doesn't mean I can't have a soft side." Cody bumped against Kennedy's chest.

"And just because I'm not thick and ripped with a bubble butt all the boys go gaga for doesn't mean I can't be strong." Kennedy pushed Cody away.

Entertained and intrigued, I stood in shocked silence and watched the argument play out.

"Did he just say 'a bubble butt all the boys go gaga for'?" Jay whispered dramatically. "Oh no he didn't." He pretended to flip his hair.

Cody and Kennedy didn't even notice.

"What the hell are we watching?" Micah turned a stunned gaze toward us before directing his attention back to Cody and Kennedy.

"If you're so strong, why don't I ever see you taking charge at the club on Sundays?" Cody challenged.

"Same reason I don't see you allowing someone else to take over," Kennedy snapped back.

"And what reason is that dare I ask?"

Cody and Kennedy were still only mere inches apart and the air crackled with the fiery tension traveling between them.

"Haven't found the right guy." Kennedy shrugged.

Cody laughed. "Nice try, Marks, but I know you're no virgin."

"Never said I was," Kennedy growled. "Just sayin' I'm not partial to taking charge unless I've got the right guy under me."

"It would take a damn miracle before I'd give in for just anyone. The day you see me submit will be a cold day in hell." Cody fisted both hands on his hips. "So, don't go getting any wild ideas that you could ever become *my* leather daddy. I need someone who can handle *all* of this." Cody gestured up and down his body.

"No worries there, Parker. I don't go for arrogant, stubborn assholes." Kennedy took a step back, his face a grimace of disdain.

I stepped between them. "As much fun as this little improv show has been, I think we've moved beyond entertaining to awkward so I suggest we all take our party outside for food and beer."

Cody and Kennedy finally broke stand off and glanced around at the rest of us as if they'd forgotten we were even there.

"What are you all staring at?" Cody grumbled.

"I don't know, boys, but it was hot as fuck." Jay fanned himself.

Leaving Kennedy and Cody to gather themselves in private, I followed the rest of the gang outside for an evening of food, drink, and fun.

Midway through our hotdogs, hamburgers, and beer, Cole nudged Jay.

"What's up with you? You seem weird." Cole cocked a brow.

"I'm a man who wears makeup and glitter, pretty sure I've always been a little *weird*." Jay sassed back.

"No, he's right, there's something different about you." Micah narrowed his eyes.

"Probably the fabulous sex." Jay tried to smartass his way out of the conversation.

Part of me was glad the guys noticed and were pushing the issue, but part of me wanted to have Jay's secret shared only between us. But, the whole group would find out what was up soon anyway, so it wasn't much of a big deal for them to hear at the same time as me.

Jay sighed and pulled a piece of paper from his pocket.

My brain took a little time to register the paper because I was expecting him to say he'd gotten another call.

Kennedy held out his hand for the paper, and I gritted my teeth against the flare of anger in the pit of my stomach. Why did Kennedy think he got to see it first?

Waiting not so patiently, I nearly ripped the sheet from his hand when Kennedy held it out for the rest of us to see.

He doesn't love you. He's not yours. You'll never belong to him. Stay away from him or you won't like what happens next.

What the actual fuck was this?

"Where did you find the note?" Kennedy immediately pulled out a notepad.

"Were you planning on keeping this secret?" I demanded before Jay could even speak.

Jay shook his head. "It was slid under my apartment door," he addressed Kennedy's question first. Turning to me, he shook his head again. "No, I wasn't going to keep it secret. I was just scared. And, today had been so great, I didn't want to ruin it." He stood and walked straight into my open arms.

"I'm sorry. It's fucking scary to walk in and find that on the floor of your home." Jay shivered in my arms.

"Shhh, it's okay. You have every right to be scared. Sort of freakin' the fuck out myself." I kissed the top of his head.

Kennedy studied the note again. "Can you grab me a baggie to stick this in?"

Micah grabbed a bag from inside and then handed it to Kennedy.

Once the evidence was bagged, Kennedy continued in full-on cop mode. "We'll see if we can get some prints, but it's unlikely we'll find anything especially since at least three of us have touched it." Kennedy shook his head in what seemed like disgust with himself and us. "Should have kept the evidence clean." Making a note on his paper, Kennedy faced Jay. "So, we're going to assume it's the same person behind the phone calls. But, I need you to think of every person you've had any kind of issues with in

the past. Old coworkers, customers, classmates, that type of thing."

Kennedy turned and pinned me with his gaze. "Who of your past lovers would be jealous and not wanting you with Jay?"

"Chill out, Barney Fife." Cody rolled his eyes and seemed to let his frustration with Kennedy simmer like a boiling pot about to blow its lid.

Kennedy turned on Cody and backed him into a tree. "Listen, Meathead, I'm an officer of the law. I need to ask questions. I could do without your comments and derision."

Cody's eyes flickered brightly in the firelight and he bit his bottom lip before giving a slight nod and pushing Kennedy away. "Go for it. Do your thing, *Officer.*"

An hour later, I watched as Kennedy took off down the hill to make a report and turn in the evidence at the station. "Dude, as much as I fear for my life to say this, I've got to say whatever *that* was between you and Kennedy was…strange?

Unexpected?" I kept an arm around Jay and spoke to my best friend.

"*That* was nothing." Cody pulled his gaze away from Kennedy's taillights as they disappeared down the hill. "*That* was proof Kennedy Marks is arrogant, stubborn, and frustrating as hell."

"Arrogant and stubborn aren't words reserved for *just* Kennedy," I hedged.

Jay drew in a quick breath and looked at me with wide eyes, his mouth forming a perfect little O.

"I'm not arrogant, I'm confident. And I'm not stubborn, I'm tenacious. Those aren't bad qualities to have," Cody grumbled as he moved around the area picking up cups and plates.

"And the sight of Kennedy in his police uniform doesn't turn you on even in the slightest?" I was pressing my luck, but Cody was fun to push sometimes.

"Any guy in uniform is fuckin' sexy as hell. But, I guarantee that Kennedy and I aren't even close to a match either personality wise or sexually." Cody tossed the trash bag into the large trashcan.

Cole cocked his head to the side. "Maybe if you two stopped arguing and getting into pissing matches every time you're around each other you'd find you actually have a lot in common."

"Or," Micah added, "maybe you'd find that your differences work well together."

Cody turned to glare at the four of us, hands on hips, nostrils flaring. "Kennedy and I would never work out. End of story. Now, how about you all get the fuck off my back?" With that, he turned and stalked to his truck.

"Bye, Papa Bear!" Jay called.

Cody gave us the finger and we all laughed.

Micah nudged me. "So, I'm guessing you guys could use some alone time." Micah grabbed Cole's hand. "We're going to pack up some more stuff from the guesthouse and take it up to the new place. You guys go settle in and take it easy."

"Thanks, that sounds great." I hugged Jay closer to my side and nodded to Micah and Cole before leading Jay to the house.

"I'm sorry I didn't tell you about the letter first thing. I wasn't going to keep it from you, I didn't want to tell you right then." Jay's eyes drooped and his voice was rough.

"Shh, that's water under the bridge now." I kissed the top of his head as we bypassed the kitchen and headed straight to my room. "The important thing is you told me, you're safe here, and the police know about the letter."

"Who is this guy? I mean, I don't think I have many enemies. Some people weren't overly fond of me back home, but I don't think anyone outright hated me, or even remembers me, or cared enough to stalk or threaten me." Jay shivered before he left my arms and grabbed his overnight bag.

I headed to the bathroom to start the shower then stood in the doorway. "Who knows? Maybe it's someone who has a history with me and doesn't want me with you?"

"But who?" Jay crinkled his nose.

I shrugged.

"What about that Nico guy? I mean, the letter didn't come until *after* you introduced me as your boyfriend and you said you've hooked up before."

Jay's suggestion was one I'd entertained for a brief moment already. "I can't rule him out completely, but he's seen me with other guys. If anything, he would be more upset with me for being with you rather than threatening you for being with me."

"Yeah, that makes sense." Jay tapped his chin. "But, we should give Kennedy the name anyway."

I nodded. "What about people at work?"

Jay leaned against the bathroom counter as the room got steamy. "I get along well with all my coworkers. Most of the customers behave. The one guy who got too handsy hasn't been back as far as I know." Jay shook his head. "I mean, I thought the calls had stopped after I asked the caller to stop and told him he was scaring me."

"Maybe the letter isn't from the same person," I suggested.

"So I'm the lucky one to get not one but two stalkers? That's just great." Jay shook his head and sighed. "I want to shower and cuddle into bed and sleep forever."

"We've got the whole weekend." I reached for the hem of Jay's shirt and lifted it over his head. "I wanted to talk to you about something."

Jay's eyes widened as he waited for what I was going to say.

"I think you should stay here until all this caller and letter mess is sorted out." I held my breath afraid Jay would balk and refuse.

"I'd like that. Going back to my apartment after finding the letter is scaring the fuck out of me." Jay's words sounded relieved as he slid his jeans and underwear down his long, lean legs.

Wow, he must really be tired and scared. That went a whole lot better than I had hoped.

Stripping off my own clothes, I threw them to the ground with Jay's. Once I'd climbed into the shower and adjusted the heat, I reached out and offered him my hand. When I'd pulled him into the steamy space and moved us both under the water, I simply held him and let the warm spray rain down on us.

CHAPTER 14

JAY

Under the spray, Levi's wet arms were a warm and safe cocoon protecting me from the world, and I could have stayed there forever, but my dick took notice of our nakedness and proximity and decided to take advantage of the situation. Levi's cock seemed totally on board with the idea and soon we were rocking our hips, our swollen lengths sliding together in slick wet heat.

"We should finish up and get you to bed," Levi whispered at my ear but his voice held no conviction.

Snaking my arms around his waist to take hold of his gorgeous ass, I wrinkled my nose. "You know, suddenly, I'm not feeling nearly as tired as I was before. It's like I got an extra boost of energy from somewhere." I thrust my cock between his legs, rubbing along his balls as his thick shaft pressed against my stomach. Squeezing the round globes of his butt, I traced a finger down his crack. "I think maybe we should make use of our shower time."

"Best idea I've heard all day." Levi grabbed the soap and lathered up his hands before handing the bar to me to do the same.

A quick but thorough washing, paying special attention to the most important parts, took place with our eyes never leaving the other. Once I was rinsed clean, I dropped to my knees and took Levi's dick in my mouth against his feeble protests.

"Wanted to suck you," Levi moaned as my tongue teased his slit and licked the underside of his head.

"You can, but me first." I returned his thick cock to my lips as I tipped up my head to meet his gaze. The fire in his eyes was enough to let me know I wouldn't be worshipping on my knees long, and that my own dick was in for a treat once I swallowed. Using my wet fingers to part Levi's ass I teased his hole with first one slick finger, then two, I reveled in his groan.

He fucked deep and hard into my mouth.

Moving one hand to fondle his balls, I sucked hard and smiled inwardly when his entire body tensed right before his release coated the back of my throat.

I'd barely licked up the last drop when Levi pulled me to my feet and maneuvered me into the corner of the shower stall.

He kissed me with warm, wet lips and thrust his tongue deeply as if to savor his taste in my mouth. "Your turn, baby." Levi dropped down and engulfed my cock with his beautiful mouth. His lips and tongue and fingers were all over my cock and balls and hole. He sucked my nut while pumping my dick with one hand and gently probing my ass with a finger. "You want my fingers in your ass?"

I could only whimper a strangled yes as I continued to rock my cock into his fist.

Slicking his already wet finger with spit, Levi teased my hole. Pressing in deeper with each passing circle of his digit, Levi patiently worked my body open.

Breathing and pushing against the sting as he breached that first tight ring, I welcomed the stinging pain that gave way to a pleasurable fullness. When his second finger joined the first, I bit my lip and tensed against the pain.

"Breath, baby. Press against me." Levi continued to stretch me open, gently grazing his fingers against the very edge of that bundle of nerves. "When my cock is in here, I'll go deep and hit that spot over and over until you see stars." He kept his fingers in my ass and pumped my cock hard and fast.

My balls drew up tight, and I exploded my release all over his lips and tongue. "Oh my god, I'm going to pass out. That was amazing, *daddy*." I threw in the nickname, knowing it would have his dick boning up again.

Levi straightened and pulled me into his arms. "Don't even think about it, you little tease. I'm washing your back and making sure the tattoo's all fixed up, and then we're going to bed. This has been an exhausting day in both good and bad ways."

I flicked my tongue against Levi's chin to lap at some of the still clinging jizz.

Levi let loose a growl from deep in his chest and captured my mouth with his. His hot, slick tongue probed deeply against mine, and I melted into his arms. If the water hadn't started getting cold, we probably would have stayed for another round.

As it was, he quickly washed my new ink and then climbed from the shower to dry off. Levi handed me a big fluffy bath towel. "I'll give you an old shirt of mine so if the fresh ink oozes it won't ruin your shirt." Levi settled me on the closed toilet seat and rubbed ointment on my tender skin before padding into his bedroom for a t-shirt. "Here, doesn't matter if this one gets stained."

I brushed my teeth while Levi checked the doors and windows. I didn't know if he always did this or if he was doing it for my sake, but I appreciated it nonetheless.

By the time I crawled under the covers, my exhaustion had come creeping back. With no more strength than a rag doll, I curled up beside Levi and sighed deeply when he pulled me into his strong, safe arms. "I'm glad we had this day together, the good and the bad," I whispered against his chest.

"I want all of your days, the good and the bad. Always." Levi kissed the top of my head. "We'll get through it all, together."

As I fell asleep, I swore that one or both of us mumbled the words *I love you*, but I may have already been dreaming.

The next morning, I stumbled into the kitchen to find Levi coming through the door with a bakery bag and two to-go beverage cups.

"Gimme, gimme." I stretched out my hands and motioned for the drinks and pastries.

"Not until you pay the fee." Levi held the items away from me and puckered his lips.

"Mmm," I hummed against his lips as I kissed him. "That's the best fee I've ever paid. Totally worth it. Now, gimme."

I took the food and drink and scurried to the counter. The scent of cinnamon wafted from the bag and the creamy spiciness of the chai latte filled the air.

Levi waited until we were halfway through breakfast before he spoke. Clearing his throat, he started. "So, this was on the front door." He pulled a paper from his pocket.

My first instinct was to panic, thinking it was another letter.

"Says you've got a certified letter to sign for at the post office." Levi handed me the postage slip.

"Jesus, Daddy. Don't do that." I held a hand to my pounding heart. "You scared the piss out of me thinking that psycho had left a letter here, too."

Levi winced. "Sorry, didn't think about that." He swigged his tea. "I'll take you down to the post office, but then we're spending the rest of the day here at home to rest and relax."

"I'll be heading back to work next week." I reminded him.

"Yeah, I know." He watched me for a few moments. "Wanted to talk to you about that. I want to be there when you work. I can stay hidden if it makes you feel better, but my gut says the phone guy and the letter guy are one and the same and both are somehow related to Strip Teaze. If I can't be there, I want one of the other guys there."

My gut reaction was to refuse, but Levi's face was etched in what looked like true fear and I knew his offer came from genuine caring. I swallowed the last bite of cinnamon roll. "That's fine. I'm okay with it." I stood to take my fork to the sink. Turning with a hand propped on my hip, I cocked my head. "But you boys better be prepared to tip and tip *well*."

Levi laughed as he walked closer and pulled me into a hug. "No worries. We wouldn't let our baby boy dance for free."

"As much as I've loved being off, I'm sort of looking forward to getting back to the routine. And I've definitely missed dancing." I snuggled against Levi's solid warmth.

"Yeah, I'm sure getting things back to normal as much as possible will feel good." He caressed my lower back. "We need to get rid of the phone calls and letters and we can really feel back to normal."

I should have known things would get bad before they got better. What was that old saying? Bad things come in three's? And, when it rains, it pours? Yeah, those two phrases came to mind once we were back up Blueridge Hill after I signed for the package at the post office.

"What do you think it is?" We sat on the couch as I examined the flat package as if it would suddenly have answers.

"Don't know. Open it. Can't be from the stalker, no one would send a certified mail letter unless they wanted to have their identity discovered." Levi nudged my elbow in encouragement.

"But, does anything good ever come in such an ominous package?" I furrowed my brow.

"*Open it* so we can find out and end the suspense." Levi bumped me with his shoulder.

"I can't. You do it." I handed the envelope to Levi.

Kissing my cheek first, Levi picked up the letter and slid a finger under the seal. "Do you want me to read it out loud or to myself first?"

"Read it to yourself before I have to hear it. Maybe you can sugar coat some of it." I had no clue why this letter had set me on edge so much, but my body shivered with anxiety.

Levi scanned the letter, shifting in his seat and glancing my way a couple times before he took a deep breath. "You want me to read the whole thing to you? Or just the gist?"

"I can tell it's not good news, so just give me the main points." I pulled my knees to my chest.

Levi dropped the letter to the ground and pulled my little fetal position ball closer to his side. "Your mother passed away."

I waited for the words to sink in, to find my heart, to fill with sadness. But I could only blink as I thought about the information. "What happened?"

"Doesn't say. Just that she passed away."

"Probably all the pills and alcohol." I wasn't sad I'd no longer see my mother, but my heart hurt at such a waste of life. "Who's it from?"

"A lawyer. Seems the mortgage company had already placed the house in foreclosure, but they wanted to offer you the chance to come take any items that might have sentimental meaning before they auction it off." Levi rubbed a hand on my shoulder.

I sat quietly for several moments. *Sentimental meaning?* Was there a single part of my life in that house or that town that had any sentimental meaning?

"Want to talk about what you're thinking?" Levi whispered.

Sitting up to face him, I gathered my thoughts. "Um," I started. "I think I'm mostly wondering what could possibly be there for me. Growing up in that house and in that town does not hold good memories, so I'm thinking it would be sort of stupid to go back."

"But?"

Levi knew me well enough to know I had more to say.

"But, the other part of me wonders if I'd always regret not going back one last time for closure. Maybe letting go of the bad memories, ya know?" A thought hit me. "Is there going to be a funeral? I'm not sure I want to be part of that."

"No, the letter says your mother expressed her wishes to be cremated with no public or private funeral." Levi remained quiet as I pondered the words.

"That's sort of sad, not living a life any friends or family would want to celebrate." My heart clenched. "I feel bad for her. She had so much potential, I mean, I'm assuming she did. Don't we all start with potential? But, her past and my father and all of her poor decisions led her down a road she wasn't able to reverse. So she died sad and alone with pills and drink as her only friends."

"Don't you dare feel guilty about any of this," Levi chided.

"No, I don't take the blame. She was messed up before she had me, I know that now that I'm older. Nothing I could have done would have saved her. I understand I had to get out of there and save myself. And, as selfish as that sounds, I'm okay with it." I sighed, my heart heavy. "But, it doesn't make the situation any better."

"That's true." Levi held me under his arm. "Can I offer my thoughts on whether or not you should go to the house?"

I nodded.

"I think you'll regret it if you don't. I think seeing the house one last time, taking anything that may hold a happy memory, saying a final goodbye to the town, I think all of those things will help you let go." Levi kissed the top of my head. "As much as the past hurts, the people and experiences made you who you are today. Maybe going back will heal your heart and be a nice big 'fuck you' to those who hurt you."

I thought about his words. "So, if you were me, would you go?"

"Yeah, I'd like to think I would. It would be hard, but I'm the type who would constantly wonder about it if I didn't take the chance to go when I could."

Having an older, more experienced man hold me and guide me was absolutely what I needed at that exact moment. "I appreciate your input and advice."

"So, do you think you want to go?"

"I think I probably should."

"Then, let's get packed and head out." Levi started to stand.

"Wait, what? I wouldn't expect you to go with me." I grabbed his hand.

"Well, you *should* expect me to go with you." Levi pulled me up from the couch. "I wouldn't send you off to do something like this on your own." He paused. "Unless you don't want me with you."

My heart soared. "Of course I want you with me. But, I can't ask you to take off work and go do something as daunting as revisiting my crappy past."

Levi wrapped his arms around my waist. "Baby boy, there's nowhere else I'd rather be. I make my own hours. I'm the boss. I can miss work. I want to help you through this. I'd love to see your past through your eyes. Maybe we'll find something good in all of the bad."

"You'd do all of that for me?" I blinked away the sting of tears.

"Of course I would," Levi whispered and then kissed me. "Want to know why?"

I nodded.

"Because I've gone and fallen so freakin' head-over-heels in love with you that I'd do anything to keep you safe, protect your heart, and keep you by my side." Levi feathered kisses all over my face.

Emotion choked me and I could no longer hold back the tears as they streamed down my cheeks. "You love me?"

Levi nodded. "I love you so much it hurts."

"I don't want it to hurt," I whispered against his lips.

"It's a good hurt." Levi assured me.

"In that case…I love you, too, *Daddy*." I smiled through our kiss causing our teeth to bump.

"This? Us? It's all proof that love doesn't make sense. Love doesn't follow rules. Love doesn't always go as planned. And you definitely can't tell love what you want. Love does whatever the hell it wants." Levi held my face in his hands. "Because never in a thousand years would I have told love that I wanted a younger, smartass twinky drama queen to hold my heart, but damn if it's not the best thing that's ever happened to me."

I laughed. "And, I definitely wouldn't have asked love to send me a sexy-as-sin, well-seasoned, sometimes grouchy, older man…oh, who the hell am I kidding? Of course I would. You, *Daddy*, are my wet dream come true."

Levi rocked me in his arms and laughed. "Only your *wet* dream come true?"

"Well, wet dreams of a man like you came first." I nuzzled my nose against his. "But, when I met you, those wet dreams turned to dreams of making you love me and spending the rest of my life with you."

"I'm sorry I made you work so hard." Levi pressed his forehead against mine. "I shouldn't have held out for so long. I'm a damn stubborn fool."

"Nah, working for it makes it all the more sweet." I closed my eyes as he kissed each lid. "And, your stubborn streak balances my drama streak perfectly."

"So, you want to pack and head out?"

"Yeah." I nodded and started toward his room. "Shit, what about work? Do you think I'll need to be gone longer than today and tomorrow?"

"Give Chuck a call. Let him know your plan is to be back by your first shift, but that you may get delayed depending on what needs to be done to finalize things at your mom's house."

Levi's advice was so sound and calming. "Good idea. Hopefully I'll be back in time, but if not, I can take a sick day or something." I grabbed my phone and called Chuck. He was extremely understanding and I thanked him profusely for allowing me the paid time off and promised to do my best to be there for my first shift back.

While I'd been talking, Levi had thrown together his overnight bag. He turned to face me. "Do you have what you need in your bag or should we head to your apartment to pick up some more things?"

"Let's run by so I can grab a few things and check the place out." I shivered at the thought of finding another letter. "You can check for letters. I don't need more of that shit right now."

"Kennedy has officers watching your apartment. I doubt the guy has left anything new." We headed toward my place. Luckily, nothing seemed out of place. I washed the little bit of dishes and smiled inwardly as Levi grabbed the sweeper to help tidy up. I had no plans of returning to the apartment anytime soon, but I wanted to leave it in good shape.

Levi must have read my mind. "Maybe you should tell your landlord you won't be renewing your lease?"

My brows shot up. "Do I have another place to live?"

Levi rolled his eyes. "Shut up. You know you do."

"Then I'll tell him he can look for another tenant." I smiled and kissed Levi's cheek before I started to throw together a few days' worth of clothes and supplies.

An hour later, we loaded up in Levi's truck and headed out of BJ.

"We'll stop for snacks in the next town." Levi patted the seat next to him.

I scooted over and then played with the radio until I found a station I liked.

"Oh lord, are you going to sing the whole ride?" Levi teased.

"Maybe, if you're lucky," I sassed back.

About twenty minutes down the road, Levi pulled into a gas station to fill up the truck. We grabbed fountain drinks, snacks, and candy for the drive.

Three hours on the road, tons of singing and laughing, and plenty of sugar and carbs, we finally reached the edge of my hometown. Patton, Indiana had never been much to look at and that definitely hadn't changed. I gave Levi final directions to my old house.

As we pulled up the drive, I noticed that any changes to the house had not been for the better. It had been crumbling, peeling, and sagging under neglect the same as me when I left, but the home was in truly bad shape now. *Home*. The word gave me pause. Was this ever really my home? No, I took shelter here and resided here, but to call it my home would be a falsehood.

"What are you thinking?" Levi grabbed my hand.

I smiled wryly. "Just that Blueridge and the BJ Boys are more my *home* than this place ever was. It's ironic that I was born here, had blood family here, and grew up here, but moving to BJ has given me real family, real roots, real love, and a real home."

"Always, baby, *always*." Levi squeezed my hand. "The lawyer is going to meet us here. You ready to get this started?"

I nodded. "The sooner we start, the sooner we get it over."

Mr. Allen, the lawyer in charge of my mom's estate pulled up the drive several moments later as Levi and I shared the porch swing.

"Mr. Owens, I'm Chris Allen, the lawyer for Steele Mortgage. I'm sorry to be meeting you under less-than-ideal circumstances." Mr. Allen held out his hand to shake.

"Nice to meet you. Call me Jay, and this is my partner, Levi Wells." The words flowed naturally and my tongue tingled with pleasure when I said them. "I wasn't at all close to my mother, so I doubt this will take long at all."

"Take as little or as much time as you need." Mr. Allen unlocked the front door and held it open for us to enter. "While going through your mother's belongings in hopes of finding next-of-kin contact information, I *did* come across something that I think you'll want to take possession of. We can discuss that later, after you've had time to go through the house."

The lawyer gestured around the front room. "Anything left here is yours for the taking, but if you don't want it, we will auction off the items along with the home to put toward the remainder of the mortgage." He moved toward the door. "I'll be doing paperwork in my car. Let me know if you need anything. I'm at your disposal five minutes, five hours, or five days from now." With a nod, Mr. Allen left Levi and me alone.

"Where do you want to start?" Levi took my hand.

I simply stared around the living room. "I have no idea."

"Let's start in the kitchen and work our way through," Levi suggested.

I nodded, unable to form coherent thoughts in that moment.

The kitchen was exactly the way I remembered. Messy, bare, worn. Not worn from years of family meals lovingly prepared in its midst. Worn from years of neglect and being used only as a storage area for prescription medications, alcohol, and junk food.

"That's the pantry where the cereal was kept." I gestured toward the open door and bare shelves. "If she forgot to leave the cereal down low, I'd pull over a chair and climb up to get a box. Took me several years to figure out how to clip the bag so the cereal didn't get stale. I loved when the boxes were new and everything would be fresh and crunchy."

Levi held me, rocking me in his arms, his front against my back.

"No kid should ever have to survive on dry cereal for days at a time." I shuddered as memories overwhelmed me. "But, part of me feels grateful I at least had that. I could have easily died if Mom hadn't had a few lucid moments of proper parenting."

"I don't know if I'd call anything she did *proper*." Levi's deep voice rumbled through me.

"There's nothing in here I want or need. But, I'm glad I saw it again. It's like I can say goodbye to that heartache." I took one last look at the kitchen as we headed to the bedrooms. "Let's do mine first." I steered us toward the little shoebox of a room in which I'd taken refuge for so many years.

The bedroom was bare. I'd taken anything I needed or wanted when I left the first time. Mom had likely sold my bed and the desk for drug money. I glanced in the built-in mirror on the wall. "God, I spent so many hours dancing in front of this mirror." I reached out and traced my hand over my glass reflection. "Sometimes the Jay in the mirror was the only friend I had."

"I'm so sorry, baby." Levi hugged me.

"No worries, the Jay in the mirror was almost as cute as me, and damn could he dance." I teased.

Levi gave me a sad smile. "Anything in here you need?"

"Nope. Just a lot of memories I'd rather bury and leave behind."

"Then say goodbye and shut the door on them." Levi stepped out of the room to give me a moment to gaze around the room.

"Bye," I whispered. Closing the door to my bedroom lifted a heaviness from my chest I hadn't even realized was there.

My mom's bedroom was a mystery to me. I wasn't ever allowed to enter her room. She spent ninety-nine percent of her life in bed. The rule was to *never* bother her when she was in that bedroom. I used to wonder if she had special secrets hidden in her room, but glancing around at that moment I saw that it was as sad and neglected as the rest of the house.

I took a step toward the bed. "I imagine this is where she died." I trailed a hand along the threadbare sheets. My heart ached as I thought of all the could have beens that were lost because of her choices. She ruined her future and tainted mine, but I vowed then and there that I would prevail over my past.

"Whatcha thinking?" Levi held my hand.

"Just that it's really good to see all of this and give it some real thought. Saying goodbye to the bad is helping me picture a future with only the good." I stepped into his space and snuggled against him as he held me.

"Looks like we only have the living room to check out. Unless you want to look at the bathroom?" Levi pulled me from the room.

I found myself drawn to the bathroom where I immediately opened the medicine cabinet. By the time I'd dug through all of the drawers, cabinets, and closets in the bathroom, I had a pile of over one hundred prescription pill bottles. "I'd like to flush all this shit, but I'm afraid it would wreck the plumbing."

"Steele Mortgage can be responsible for making sure it's disposed of properly." Levi kicked at the bottles with the toe of his shoe. "I don't know that I've ever seen this many bottles in one place."

"Yeah, Mommy Dearest had her own little pharmacy." I shook my head. "Want to know the irony? The few times I can ever remember being sick, she *never* had anything to give me and refused to 'waste money' on a doctor. For as small and neglected as I was, I feel blessed I wasn't sick more than a few times."

"Living room?" Levi seemed antsy and ready to get out of the house, or at least away from my bad memories.

I walked into the living room behind him. My eyes fell on the couch and I couldn't keep the smile from my lips. "There's one thing I *do* want." I walked to the sofa and picked up the soft blanket. Holding it to my nose and breathing deeply, I sighed. "My grandma gave this to my mom when I was born. I used to carry it around the house, sleep with it, and use it as my shield." I looked at the worn cloth. "It's seen better days, but I want to take this."

Levi nodded and ran a hand over my old blanket. "What about any of the furniture?"

"Nah, none of it is any good or holds anything but bad memories." I shook my head. "Plus, my new roommate is a bit stodgy and would throw a fit if I brought something into his house that didn't match his manly décor."

Levi laughed. "You're not wrong."

We headed out the door to meet with Mr. Allen just under an hour later.

Closing the door on that house and those memories was the most therapeutic thing I'd done in my entire life.

"Thanks for making me come. And thanks for coming with me." I hooked my arm with Levi's, and we met the lawyer at the picnic table at the side of the house.

CHAPTER 15

LEVI

Jay took the package from Mr. Allen as we sat in the sunshine at the picnic table.

My eyes widened in surprise.

"She did *what*?" Jay's words held the same astonishment I was feeling.

"I found this letter and envelope when I was looking for contact information. The letter and package are addressed to you." Mr. Allen cleared his throat. "Please forgive me for reading the letter, but it wasn't sealed and I was hoping for an address or something."

Jay pulled the letter from the envelope and stared at it for several moments, not seeming to read, just staring.

"Do you need anything else from us?" Jay asked Mr. Allen abruptly.

"No, I'll lock the house back up and be on my way." The lawyer shook our hands. "Thank you both for coming so quickly. I'll be glad to get this one closed."

After that brief goodbye, we climbed into the truck. Jay never spoke a word, just stared at the letter and clutched the package. I made an executive decision that we weren't going back to BJ that night. I turned the truck toward Indianapolis, Indiana. My boy and I were going to spend the night in the big city before we headed back home.

Two hours later, Jay had dropped the letter and package and curled up on my lap sound asleep. When I pulled into the hotel's parking lot, I hated to wake him, but knew I had to. "Hey baby, want to go inside?"

Jay sat up and looked around. "Where are we?"

"Thought we could use the night to sight see and relax in Indy. You up for it?" I raised my brow in question.

Jay smiled and nodded. "Definitely."

We checked into the Sheraton Inn and immediately tossed down our bags, toed off our shoes, and climbed into bed.

Jay clutched the letter and package to his chest.

"Want to open it?" I was dying to know what was in the envelope, but I knew Jay needed to process and open it in his own time.

"Yeah. But, can you read the letter to me? I've read it to myself a couple times, but I can't believe it. I need to hear it come from someone else's mouth." Jay handed me the letter.

I nodded and unfolded the paper. Clearing my throat, I began to read one of the most heart wrenching, beautifully maddening messages of all time.

My dearest Jay,

I am sorry. Those are the simplest yet most profound words I could ever say to you. I failed you. Not only as a mother, but as a person as well. And for that, I am truly sorry.

I didn't plan on having kids. I knew I was way too messed up to raise another human being. But, I was so excited when I found out you were coming. I regret deeply that I wasn't able to overcome my addictions to care for you in the way you needed and deserved.

My heart broke AND rejoiced the day you left home. I hurt to know I'd likely never see my beautiful boy ever again. But, I knew it was for the best. I knew you needed to rid yourself of this town and of me if you were ever going to heal and overcome your past. I pray that moving away provided the love, comfort, and belonging that you so desperately deserve.

Thank you for the money. The first time you sent it, I fell to my knees in shock and sadness. I needed that money. I could have spent every single cent you ever mailed on drinking and pills. But, I knew I wouldn't. I couldn't. I know I failed you, I neglected you, and I prayed I hadn't ruined you, but I knew the one thing I COULD do was provide you with a small nest egg upon my death. So, every month that you sent money, I holed it away. I was never able to overcome my addiction, but I was determined to live up to my love for you. I know you never had concrete proof that I loved you, but I did, I loved you so much. But, my past and my issues were stronger and I was weak. But, one thing that kept me going some days was waiting for the money I came to expect from you each month. Setting it aside and saving it was my way of being able to show you, maybe for the only time in your life, that your mother loves you.

I'm sorry. It's so small, but those words are the gospel truth. I live daily with the guilt of what I did to you. I'm sorry my love wasn't visible. I'm sorry my addiction controlled me. I'm sorry I wasn't enough. I pray that you are happy, loved, and safe. That's all I've ever wanted for you. I hope the money can help in some way.

In love and sorrow,
Mom

I finished reading the letter and sat in stunned silence with Jay curled in my arms.

"Whoa, I don't even know what to say." I ran a hand down Jay's arm. "You want to talk about all of that?"

Jay shook his head. "No, I think I need time to process. I mean, the money is great, but I would give it all back if it meant having a normal childhood and knowing my mom loved me."

"I know you would, babe." I kissed the top of his head.

"But, I feel guilty thinking this, I probably would have never moved to BJ or met you or the guys if I'd grown up loved and cared for." Jay shivered in my arms.

The thought of that was like an arrow to my heart. I longed for Jay to have known a happy, safe childhood, but thinking about him never coming to BJ and becoming such an important part of my life hurt deep inside my chest. "Shhh, it's okay. We can't change the past, but we can make our future what we want it to be." I rocked Jay in my arms. "What do you want for the future?"

"I want you, a comfortable and safe life, possibly with children someday, and the circle of friends we have in BJ." Jay's words were determined. "And I want to do something to help kids who have crappy childhoods. Give them someplace to go when they need to escape. I don't know what yet, but that's what I want to do."

"Then that's what we'll do." My heart filled to near bursting to hear Jay's words. "Are you going to open the package?"

Jay shook his head. "No, if she saved everything I sent I know about how much is in there. I'll take it to the bank once we're home."

"Okay, but I think it's likely better to lock the money in my truck." I took the package from him and stretched us out on the bed. "Do you want to go explore the city? Or would you rather nap? Either way, I figure we'll find a place for dinner and drinks later."

Jay seemed to mull over my question for several seconds. "How about we shower, take a short nap, explore, and then grab dinner and drinks?"

"That sounds absolutely fabulous." I kissed his head before rolling from bed. "I'll turn the shower on. You go first and I'll look up some things we might want to see. Maybe we'll ask some locals for food and drink recs."

"Want to share the shower to conserve water?" Jay waggled his brow.

"Yes, but no. We'll save that for later. If we start now, we'll never leave the room." I gave him a shove and sent him toward the hot shower. "Save me some water."

By the time Jay exited the bathroom, I'd found a couple things we might want to see. "Seems like there are *a lot* of things to do and see in Indy. We'll have to plan another trip up here to take it all in."

Jay was sound asleep by the time I finished my shower and climbed into bed with him. Setting the bedside alarm for one hour, I pulled him into my arms. "I love you," I whispered as sleep overtook me.

"I think we could spend a week here and not see everything there is to see." Jay cuddled beneath my arm as we traveled around the center of Indy's downtown in a horse-drawn carriage. "I definitely think we should come back."

Our hour nap had refreshed us enough to walk to the White River State Park and Downtown Canal Walk. We saw the edge of the Indianapolis Zoo and Butterfly Garden, which were definites on the return-to-see list.

Tonight, we had plans to see Massachusetts Avenue and then head to Metro Nightclub for dinner and drinks. We'd asked at the hotel and Mass Ave was highly recommended for shopping fun, eclectic little shops, and seeing artwork. Metro was supposedly one of the top gay bars in the city with great food and drinks.

By the time we arrived at Metro, we were both dragging. Mass Ave was said to be "forty-five degrees from ordinary" and we loved every inch of it. But, Jay and I were both exhausted.

"We are so totally taking a cab or Uber back to the hotel," Jay grumbled before turning a dazzling smile toward the man who greeted us. "Well, hello."

"Welcome to Metro. You boys want a seat at the bar, a table, or out on the patio?"

I glanced around the packed establishment. "Which gets us a seat the quickest?"

Our host, Chet, consulted a list. "I've got a table inside open now."

"We'll take it."

"And water, please. Lots of water." Jay fanned his face.

Once Chet had us seated, he left.

We perused the menu and an equally attractive waiter appeared with our waters.

"There's so much to choose from," Jay muttered as he studied the menu.

"Everything here is delicious," a man from a neighboring table offered. "Seriously, I don't think I've ever ordered anything I didn't love."

"That's because you love food, period." His companion piped up.

Jay and I laughed and agreed that everything on the menu did look amazing.

"I'm Braeton and this is my husband, Drew. We're regulars here and locals to Indy. We can tell you all the best and worst places in town." Braeton held out his hand to shake, and Drew followed suit.

"I'm Levi and this is my boyfriend, Jay."

We shook hands all around.

"Are you guys new to Indy?" Drew inquired.

"No, just visiting for the day. We're on an impromptu excursion, leaving tomorrow. But, we will definitely be back. It's a gorgeous city." I noticed immediately the similarities between Jay and me and the couple seated next to us. *Opposites attract* was clearly alive and well.

"Here, let me give you my card. When you're back in town, text me, and Drew and I will act as tour guides." Braeton pulled a card from his pocket and handed it over. "And, as weird as it sounds, feel free to skip the hotel and stay with us. We've got the room and it will save you money."

Drew's eyes bugged out as his husband spoke. "Excuse him. He's never really met a stranger. We don't usually invite strangers to sleep in our home within five minutes of meeting them."

"What? Look at them. They are totally trustworthy. I'm a great judge of character. Seriously, I don't think gay axe murderers frequent the Metro, so we're safe." Braeton sassed his husband before turning back to Jay and me. "Seriously though, we love Indy, and we've got amazing friends here. Let us know when you'd like to visit again and we'll help you make plans."

"And, you *are* totally welcome to stay with us if you'd like," Drew added. "Here's my card, as well."

Braeton and Drew finished their drinks and paid their bill while continuing small talk with us.

"We'd love to stay and chat, but we've got theater tickets with friends this evening." Drew slid his wallet into his back pocket.

They stood, shook our hands, and said goodbye.

By the time we were ready to leave, Jay was convinced that Metro had the best bar food he'd ever eaten. He was also quite tipsy on the four drinks he'd guzzled.

"We'll take the check, please." I motioned to our waiter, Scott.

"Your check has been taken care of." Scott winked and smiled.

"What? Who did that? That was soooo sweet," Jay purred.

"Braeton and Drew wanted to treat you to dinner and drinks," Scott explained.

"Awww, now we definitely need to come back to Indy to hang out with our new friends." Jay giggled. "I need the powder room." He hiccupped.

"Oh, lord. Do you think you can make it on your own?" I laughed.

"Yes, Daddy, I think I can manage." Jay sashayed his way to the men's room while I wandered to the door to wait for him.

"Hope you'll come back to Indy and Metro. Thanks for coming in today." Chet waved goodbye as he took another party to their table.

Once I got Jay into an Uber, I was grateful we weren't driving back to BJ that night or super early. Ten minutes later, the car pulled up at the Sheraton and I hooked arms with Jay as we entered the building.

Upstairs, in the privacy of our room, I kissed him. "You are absolutely gorgeous, and I love you more than you will ever know. I want an infinite number of days like this with you."

"Mmm, I love you, too." Jay bit my lip and then soothed the sting with his tongue. "Can tonight be the night?"

"What night?" I pulled away and looked at Jay, confused.

"The night you finally take me and make me fully yours?" Jay blushed. "I want you to top me. Please?"

Every drop of blood in my body shot straight to my dick and every thought of heading to bed to get a good night's sleep flew from my mind.

"God, baby, yes. If you think that's what you want and you're ready, then fuck yes." I kissed Jay's beautiful pink lips.

"Well, give me a little time alone in the bathroom, but I'm hoping the butt plug I've been walking around with in my ass all day has helped to make sure I'm ready." Jay smiled evilly before he sauntered to the bathroom and shut the door behind him.

"Holy fuck." I forced my lungs to take a deep breath and blew it out slowly. Jay had used a butt plug. For me. He'd had it in, stretching his body, *for me*.

Shit. If I let myself think about it too much, I'd bust a nut before he was even out of the bathroom. I listened absentmindedly as the water ran in the sink, the toilet flushed, and the shower started. When Jay cracked the door, I jumped.

"Heya, Daddy, want to join me in a quick wash?" He swung the door open all the way to reveal his sleek, lean, and very naked body—his very aroused naked body.

Fuuuck.

I stripped my clothes on the way to the bathroom.

I followed Jay into the shower and quickly took control. Pressing his chest to the tile, I grabbed his cock and pumped while thrusting my hard length against his ass. "This what you want, baby?" My words may have come out strong and confident, but my insides were goo at the thought of giving Jay his first time. I would have died before anyone else got to be his first, but I was scared to death I'd mess up somehow.

Jay whimpered and pumped his cock into my fist. "God, yes. Please."

"Not here. Wash. I want you in a bed." I grabbed the soap and slicked his body before lathering my own.

When Jay plastered his soapy body against mine and our slick dicks connected, I nearly wept. Reaching for his ass and grabbing a handful, I traced my finger along his crack. "You still have the plug in?"

Jay bit his lip and nodded. "Took it out to do a thorough cleaning, but I put it back in. It feels so good, but I want it to be you."

"Fuck, baby, when you say things like that…," I groaned against his ear as my finger found the edge of the plug.

"What? Does it make you hot?"

"Damn straight it does. Now, rinse off and get in the bed." I washed the soap from my body and climbed out to dry off. Leaving Jay to finish rinsing, I left the bathroom to rummage in my bag for a condom and lube. My hands trembled as I placed the items on the bedside table.

"You ready for me, Daddy?" Jay purred as he walked up behind me and wrapped his slender arms around my waist to tickle his fingers at the base of my dick.

I turned him around and pushed him to the bed. Leaning over him, my weight supported on my shaking arms, I paused to catch my breath.

"You okay? Why are you shaking?" Jay ran his hands up my arms.

"I want this so damn much, but I'm so damn scared I'll mess it up." I choked on the emotion of having the man I loved under me, waiting for me to make love to him.

"You could never mess up. Even if we roll over and go to sleep right now, it's the best I've ever had." Jay wiggled himself to a better position on the bed. "I've never done this, so I have nothing to compare it to."

"That's not exactly comforting," I snorted before leaning in to kiss him.

"It will be perfect because it's you." Jay kissed me back.

"Can I play with you?" I teased my finger around the plug.

"Yes, but not for long. We'll have to work on building up my stamina. Too much playing and I'll be out before the main event." Jay relaxed into the mattress and closed his eyes as I slid the plug out of his body. Slicking it with lube, I pressed the device against his hole again and groaned as he opened to take it in inch by inch.

"Fuck, that's good," Jay whispered.

"You're so fucking beautiful." I twirled and teased the plug in and out a few more times. "Baby, I need this to be my cock before I come all over the sheets." I left the plug in to continue stretching Jay's tight ring while I rolled the condom down my throbbing length and doused it with a good amount of lube. Drizzling the liquid onto Jay's ass, I slowly pulled the plug from his body. "Shhh," I assured him when he whimpered at the loss. "I'll give you something so much better."

Moving Jay's hips to the edge of the bed, I placed his calves on my shoulders and lined up the head of my cock with his hole. Pressing against his most sensitive flesh, I ground my teeth to keep from crying out at the slow agonizing pleasure of his hot body stretching open and sheathing my dick.

"Holy shit. Thank god for the butt plug. It was tight and felt good. But you're huge and feel amazing. I'm glad I wore that all day or my poor ass would be ruined." Jay panted and gripped his weeping cock.

"I'm not going to last long watching you fuck your hand and with your tight little ass squeezing me, so I'm going to fuck you until you come. Then I'm going to pull out and paint myself all over your body." I left no room for argument or protest and began to thrust slow and deep into Jay's heat.

Jay pressed up on his elbows to watch my cock invade his body over and over.

I knew the moment I hit his prostate because he screamed and tensed right before his release shot all over his chest and stomach.

Pulling from him slowly, I made quick work of removing the condom and took my pulsing length in my fist.

Jay rolled up to a sitting position and kissed me while I pumped my cock. When his tongue swept through my mouth and his hand cupped my balls, I knew I was a goner. With a deep roar, I painted my release into his and rejoiced as he ran his fingers through the stickiness of our combined pleasure.

Pressing him back to the mattress, I collapsed on top of him. "You okay? Was I too rough?"

"I'm so much better than okay. If I died right this second, I could die a happy man." Jay rolled his head back and moaned as his body shivered at the kisses I planted on his neck. "I'm not sure there's a 'too rough,' but I'll be glad to experiment to see if we ever find that point."

I laughed. "That sounds like the perfect plan." I reached to the floor and grabbed a towel. Wiping our bodies clean, I tossed the towel toward the bathroom.

"These past two days have been ridiculously up and down." Jay cuddled into my side as I pulled the blankets over us. "Finishing my tattoo, moving in with you, hearing that you love me, exploring Indy and making new friends, and having the best sex of my life are all rating pretty high on the amazing scale."

"What about the bad?"

"Well, having Nico proposition me, some psycho leaving a threatening letter, finding out that my mom died, and having to travel back to a town I'd hoped to never see again are all pretty high on the suck-o-meter."

"Surely we've had enough lows for now. Maybe we can accumulate some more highs to even it out." I murmured into Jay's silky hair.

"The good already outweighs the bad." Jay tipped up his head to kiss my chin. "Thank you for everything. I love you."

"Love you so damn much." I grabbed his face and devoured his mouth.

I had every intention of checking my phone for texts or turning on the television for some news, but I drifted into sleep and didn't wake until late the next morning.

I woke to an incessant buzzing. Clearing the sleep fog from my head, I finally realized it was my phone making the noise. Grabbing the phone, I accepted the call from Kennedy.

"Hello?"

"Levi, Jay's with you, right?" Kennedy barked.

"Yeah, he's right here." I looked toward my beautiful boy sharing the bed and saw his eyes on me.

"What's wrong?" Jay mouthed.

I shrugged. "What's up?" I didn't take my eyes off Jay as I spoke to Kennedy.

"We've got a development in Jay's case. Are you guys coming home today?"

"Yeah, probably leaving here within two hours. But, you can't expect us to drive all that way without some more details." I frowned and reached for Jay's hand and turned the phone on speaker. "Jay can hear you now. Go ahead."

"Well, the caller turned himself in and outed the letter writer. The caller had technically done nothing illegal, and he was on his way out of town for good, so we let him go in a trade for telling us who left the threatening letter." Kennedy's voice held strength and pride.

"Seriously? That's great. So who were the guys?"

"From what we can gather, and Jay will have to confirm all of this once you guys are back in BJ and come to the station, we know the perpetrator was the guy who got way too handsy after the breakup with his longtime boyfriend. The longtime boyfriend was the one who wrote the letter." Kennedy paused. "Jay, you need to decide if you want to press charges against the letter guy. He's provided us with the name and address of where he's moving to if you don't press charges. He'll have to stick around here if you press charges."

"I don't want to press charges. I want them gone and all of it over and done with." Jay squeezed my hand.

"We can take care of all of that," Kennedy assured Jay.

"So, what made the guy turn himself in and turn on his lover?" I was relieved it was all looking to be over soon, but my mind still wondered about how it all started and what led to it ending.

"Handsy said he had never meant to hurt or scare Jay, just found himself feeling very drawn to him. As soon as Jay told him he was scared, the caller realized he'd messed up and stopped calling. But, by then, he and his ex had started working things out and the ex found out about how much Handsy was drawn to Jay. Handsy said his ex got obsessed and started making plans to really hurt Jay. When the ex told Handsy about the threatening letter, and his plan to attack Jay after his first night back at Strip Teaze, Handsy freaked out. Moved all of his stuff to a new place at least an hour from BJ then came back to tell us what he knew."

"What about the letter guy?" I didn't like the fact that this man had plans worked out in his head to hurt Jay.

"He broke down and admitted to the letter when we hinted we knew about it and his plans. We can hold him if you're going to press charges. Or, we've got his name and new address plus the name of his new employer in a state at least a day's drive from BJ. I'll have the local authorities keep an eye on him and make contact with his boss to be sure he stays away." Kennedy paused. "Unless you decide you want to file charges?"

Jay shook his head. "No, I want it over and done so we can move on."

We ended the call with Kennedy, showered, and packed up.

We climbed into the truck after checking out of the hotel.

"So I guess I don't need to move in with you now." Jay bit his lip.

"The fuck you say. That part isn't changing at all." I reached for his hand. "Unless you truly don't want to move in with me?"

"No, I want to. As long as you're okay with it."

"Definitely." I squeezed his hand. I drove in silence, enjoying Jay's hand in mine.

"Can we stop for breakfast? I'm starving." Jay batted his long lashes.

"Yes, we can stop. I've got to keep my bottomless pit filled." I laughed.

"I feel there are way too many sexual jokes that I could make right now, and I've not had enough caffeine for that, so I'm going to pretend that your comment wasn't just laced with innuendo." Jay rolled his eyes.

"Only you could make something dirty out of a breakfast comment." I shook my head and pulled him close to me on the seat of the truck.

"Don't deny that you love it." Jay sassed.

"I did my best to deny it, but I love you and I love that sassy mouth of yours." I kissed him, tracing my tongue over his lips.

"Can't fight true love." Jay shrugged as we drove toward BJ arm-in-arm.

EPILOGUE

JAY

I stood to the side and listened to Micah and Cole recite their wedding vows while never once taking my eyes from Levi standing across from me.

"I love you," he mouthed, and I returned the sentiment.

Two years was a long time to wait for a guy, but I've never once regretted it. Levi is my one, my only, my dream come true.

Once my caller and stalker were out of the picture, Levi and I settled into a very comfortable routine filled with fun, laughter, amazing sex, and lots of love. Yeah, I know I got out of the whole psycho stalker thing pretty easy, but what can I say? Maybe I'm magic?

I used the money my mom gave me to travel to dance camp for six weeks. It was the longest six weeks of my life away from Levi, but I learned a shit ton and gained a lot of dancing and teaching experience. The rest of the money got put in the bank for safekeeping while Levi and I worked out the plans for The Blue Jay.

The Blue Jay will be how I help kids. It will be opened and staffed twenty-four seven to provide dance, art, and music classes along with counseling, tutoring, and mentoring. It's not up and running yet, but our plans are coming along nicely. If I'd had a place like that to go when I was younger, a place to escape the bad and focus on the good, maybe things wouldn't have sucked so much. My goal is to make things a little easier on kids who are having a rough time.

I recognize the irony in the whole situation. My mom is the reason my childhood sucked. But, my mom is also the reason I'm able to provide assistance to other kids at The Blue Jay. So, in a way, my mom caused my suffering and allowed my dream to come true at the same time. That's sort of a mind fuck.

Until we get The Blue Jay up and running, I'm dancing once a month at Strip Teaze. I'm the headliner, how cool is that? And I'm teaching dance classes which I'll move to The Blue Jay once it opens. I'm also doing part time choreography for the high school theater club and dance team.

Levi's tattoo shop has gotten so busy that he had to hire another artist for the small pieces, piercings, and walk-ins. Levi does the large works and by appointment only.

Micah and Cole are obviously doing fabulously since they are getting married and even talking about adopting a kid. Cody and Kennedy have yet to admit they are hot for each other, but I have a feeling the rest of us are going to snap one day and finally force them to get together even if it's just to fuck each other's brains out so they can stop arguing and fighting every damn time we're together.

"I now pronounce you Mr. and Mr. You may kiss your husband." The officiant's words broke through to my wandering mind. The heat of Levi's gaze pulled mine back to his. As Micah and Cole shared their first kiss as married men, I started dreaming of my own wedding.

Wonder what Levi would think of pink glitter? I know my man, if I want a pink glitter wedding, he may protest, but he won't fight me too much. And, I don't mind a little resistance. True love is worth the fight.

FROM THE AUTHOR

Don't miss my other male/male romance books in the Something About Him series! author.to/ADEllisAmazon

THANK YOU FOR READING! I hope you enjoyed; please take a moment to leave a review. If you're reading on a file/device that doesn't take you to a review option, please consider finding the book on the platform of your choice and giving a star rating and a short review. It doesn't have to be long and drawn out, just a few sentences about how it made you feel, what you liked/didn't like. THANK YOU!!

If you are interested in my male/female contemporary romance series (Torey Hope) or my other male/male romance books, please check out my website to find information about all of my books. Or, search your favorite book platform for my name and see if something tickles your fancy.

A.D. Ellis

ABOUT THE AUTHOR

A.D. Ellis is an Indiana girl, born and raised. She spends much of her time in central Indiana teaching alternative education in the inner city of Indianapolis, being a mom to two amazing school-aged children, and laughing at a precocious cat. A lot of her time is also devoted to phone call avoidance and her hatred of cooking.

She loves chocolate, wine, pizza, and naps along with reading and writing romance. These loves don't leave much time for housework, much to the chagrin of her husband of nearly two decades. Who would pick cleaning the house over a nap or a good book? She uses any extra time to increase her fluency in sarcasm.

FREE books-- sign up at bit.ly/ADEllisNews for a FREE male/female romance. Sign up at http://www.subscribepage.com/ADEllisNewsMMR omance for a FREE male/male romance book.

Facebook www.facebook.com/adellisauthor

Twitter www.twitter.com/ADEllisAuthor

Website http://adellisauthor.com/

ACKNOWLEDGEMENTS

This is always one of the hardest parts of finishing a book, but quite possibly the most important part! It's so hard because I fear I'll miss someone who has helped me out, supported me, been a listening ear, or offered advice and encouragement. If I miss listing your name here, please know it wasn't on purpose, and I love you dearly!

A dear friend once again made this book possible. I'm not sure he understands how much his input means to me and how he shapes my stories with his words, answers, experiences, and heart. Thank you, Brett, as always. Don't ever doubt your potential and how lucky people are to know you.

And, to Gage. You are truly an amazing person. Thank you, again, for all of your help and input. Not to get all mushy, but you have an incredible future ahead of you because you can do absolutely anything you set your mind to. And, I feel blessed to get to watch you reach the stars.

To David, Donny, Kurt, and Chris- your input on this book meant a lot and was very much appreciated. Thank you all!

To my friend, fellow author, and cover designer, Kay Simone at <u>Kay Simone Creative</u>. Thank you for listening to my vision and making it beautiful! You are a superb talent and I'm lucky to call you my designer.

To Jill, thank you for ripping this story apart and helping me to build it back to something readers can enjoy.

To my dear beta readers. Your input, feedback, and encouragement has proven invaluable to me! I truly trust you all and value your opinions more than you'll probably ever understand. Thank you to my newest betas as well. When I needed fresh new eyes who had never read any of these characters you were there for me and helped me so much!

To my Ellis Elite Private Discussion Group— THANK YOU! Those of you who list me in contests and comments and shout outs all the time, you're amazing and I love you for always working to get my name out there! If I start naming people here, I'll be sure to miss some; just know if you've ever shared my name or my books, it means the world to me and I appreciate you more than you'll ever know!

To my READERS!! You are what keeps me going. You are the reason I write some days. When I don't feel like I have it in me, I'll get a message or comment from a reader about how a story of mine has touched them, and *that* will be the inspiration and motivation for me to write. As long as these stories are in my head, I'll keep sharing them with you.

To the BLOGGERS who read and review and share my books!! You are beyond a shadow of a doubt some of the most dedicated and selfless people I've ever known! Thank you so much for being such a support to those of us who have stories to tell. I love BLOGGERS!

To my Juice Box ladies! Thank you so much for welcoming me into your crew and sharing your knowledge, experience, advice, and fun with me!

Having some real-life authors/friends I can collaborate with is a great feeling. Dance parties, lunches, movies, videos, wine, painting, pizza, sushi, cookies…the list goes on and on! Thank you for letting me be a Juice Boxer!

To my MM Slack group who helped with the blurb for this story, thank you much for the advice and support.

To my fellow authors. Those of you who read my work, share your work with me, cross-promote with me, and offer advice and support, THANK YOU! You make this a little easier and enjoyable.

To my family and friends. I know most of you don't understand my obsession with getting these stories out of my head and on paper, but you're proud of me either way. Some of you get to read my books, some of you get to see cover ideas, some of you have to watch me lose myself in a story, some of you have to hear me vent about the hard parts of all of this; all of you love me and support me and for that, I am truly lucky and grateful.

CONNECT WITH A.D. ELLIS

Follow my website http://www.adellisauthor.com or find me on Facebook http://www.facebook.com/adellisauthor

If you want updates about releases, interviews, sales, giveaways, and more please sign up for my newsletter bit.ly/ADEllisNews

You can also find me on Twitter http://www.twitter.com/ADEllisAuthor

Find me on Spotify if you'd like to listen to my playlists (mainly the songs I listened to while writing). Just search for A.D. Ellis.